DRAWING DEAD

A Chase Adams FBI Thriller
Book 3

Patrick Logan

Books by Patrick Logan

Detective Damien Drake

Book 1: Butterfly Kisses
Book 2: Cause of Death
Book 3: Download Murder
Book 4: Skeleton King
Book 5: Human Traffic
Book 6: Drug Lord: Part One
Book 7: Drug Lord: Part Two

Dr. Beckett Campbell, ME

Book 0: Bitter End
Book 1: Organ Donor
Book 2: Injecting Faith

The Haunted Series

Book 1: Shallow Graves
Book 2: The Seventh Ward
Book 3: Seaforth Prison
Book 4: Scarsdale Crematorium
Book 5: Sacred Heard Orphanage
Book 6: Shores of the Marrow
Book 7: Sacrifice

This book is a work of fiction. Names, characters, places, and incidents in this book are either entirely imaginary or are used fictitiously. Any resemblance to actual people, living or dead, or of places, events, or locales is entirely coincidental.

Copyright © Patrick Logan 2018
Interior design: © Patrick Logan 2018
All rights reserved.

This book, or parts thereof, cannot be reproduced, scanned, or disseminated in any print or electronic form.

First Edition: August 2019

Prologue

AS WAS HER HABIT, Chase observed her opponents as they glanced at their cards rather than immediately looking at her own. This wasn't a unique tactic; in fact, it was fairly common especially among players of this caliber. After all, once a person became aware that there were eyes on them, they fell into a transient, almost meditative state from which very little information could be gleaned. But Chase found that when players first looked at their cards, the small dopamine they received affected their irises, their blink rate, and caused the corners of their mouths to move ever so slightly.

There were six players at the table, including herself. A Russian diplomat who went by the singular name 'Mishenko,' Tim Tigner, the young CEO of an up and coming file sharing platform, Deb Koch, a divorcee of a Texan oil baron, and two online pros: Steven Darwish and a man who went by the incredibly cheesy nickname, *The Guru*.

So far as she could tell over the course of the six-hour session, the players at the table were only interested in their cards and the twelve to fourteen million dollars at stake.

None of them seemed capable of murder; not yet, anyway. But the night was still young.

Chase watched as Tim Tigner looked down at his cards and then quickly tossed them into the muck. It was a routine enough act, one fueled by muscle memory no less, but there were subtle differences. On one occasion, his folded cards had collided with a stack of bills and flipped over, revealing a king and a ten of clubs. In this particular case, Chase had noticed that Tim's thumb had lingered just a moment longer on the top card as he tossed them, which had caused their trajectory to be shorter than intended. It wasn't much information and could have just been a fluke, but Chase knew better than to ignore this. The alternative was that when Tim folded a mediocre hand, he held the cards differently.

The next two players to act were the online professionals, who Chase gathered were using this high-stakes private game as a testing ground before branching out to more mainstream live events. Their playing style was reminiscent of her own: tight/aggressive. And yet, every so often, about once an hour, Chase surmised, they played loose/aggressive with subpar hands. Throughout the evening, they had remained cool and composed, never getting too high or too low, irrespective of how the game played out in front of them.

And it had served them well: both had healthy stacks of bills in front of them.

The first online pro, Steven Darwish, made a standard raise of 60k.

Chase watched the next player, The Guru, closely as he ruminated over his decision. This had proved difficult for her; not *just* reading the player for insight into their cards but reading the player *and* trying to figure out which one of them might be capable of murder.

The second to last thing she wanted was to lose two million dollars that wasn't hers.

The last thing she wanted was to become a victim in another poker massacre.

The Guru tossed his cards into the muck and Mishenko quickly called.

And now the action was on her.

Chase flipped up the top corners of her cards and glanced at them briefly before lowering them to the felt again.

"One-hundred and fifty," she announced, moving three stacks of 50k toward the center of the table. It was a standard raise, one and a half times Darwish's bet, one that she hoped would bump Mishenko from the hand.

As Chase suspected, Darwish flat called. It was Mishenko who acted out of character. The man had been playing extremely tight for the last hour, and she had suspected that he was going to fold.

He didn't; Mishenko called, bringing the pot up to nearly half-a-million dollars, with the blinds and antes considered. It was one of the bigger pre-flop pots of the night, and Chase felt her heart rate increase slightly.

Control, she whispered in her head. *Remain in control, Chase.*

Even though an hour before the game had started the prospect of sitting down at the table with two million dollars was unfathomable, the stacks of bills were in front of her now.

Which made them her responsibility.

Control.

But when the flop came and the bullets started flying moments later, her thoughts changed.

While Chase's drive was still ultimately singular, it had transformed from *control* to *survive*.

Survive, Chase, for the love of God, survive.

PART I – Recovery

FORTY-EIGHT HOURS AGO

Chapter 1

"I'M NOT TAKING IT," Chase Adams said as she stared at the blue tab nestled at the bottom of the plastic cup. "I don't need it."

Nurse Whitfield stared at Chase, her thin lips pressed together tightly, but she refrained from responding. This unnerved Chase even more than when she'd instructed her to swallow the damn methadone tab.

"I'm not taking it," Chase repeated.

This time, the nurse spoke up.

"Chase, come on, please. You know you have to take it."

Chase lowered her eyes to the blue tab again, her lip curling in disgust.

"You need to take it, Chase. It'll make you feel better."

Chase scoffed.

The methadone didn't make her feel better at all; it made her feel like shit. And by some strange paradoxical irony, given that the drug was designed as a less toxic replacement for the former, it worked the *opposite* of heroin, at least for Chase.

Heroin made her memories go away.

Methadone caused them to come roaring back in full force.

But this wasn't something that she felt like sharing, especially not with the nurse.

Fuck, she thought, still staring at the innocuous blue tab. Now she regretted raising a stink; Nurse Whitfield would be watching her even more intently.

"Please, Chase," the nurse repeated. She was a nice enough woman and had always treated Chase with respect and yet, at that moment, Chase loathed her. "We can speak to the doctor if you want to change the dose, but you know the protocol. You have to book an appointment, and you have to continue to take your meds until you see him."

Four months, Chase thought sourly. *Four months I've been squirreled away with crackheads and other lowlife delinquents, listening to them blather on about their problems* ad nauseum.

And yet, the worst part, by a large margin, was the methadone.

When Chase had first arrived at Grassroots Recovery, the doctor had commended her on her physical appearance, something that she attributed to her running, but warned that while she looked good on the outside, her insides were in rough shape.

Especially the insides of her skull.

The shaking had started shortly thereafter, something that Chase thought she was mentally prepared for. Her initial outlook was *not* to medicate, but when a nurse found her soaked in her own sweat, locked in the fetal position and moaning uncontrollably, the doctor had quickly prescribed her 50mg of methadone. Chase had reluctantly taken the meds and had been comforted by a momentary reprieve from the physical and psychological anguish.

But this didn't last long.

Chase had tried to doze off an hour or so after taking the meds, which quickly proved unwise. Almost immediately, she was visited by some old friends, old friends that she wished never to see again: the man in the van sporting faded blue overalls, Agent Martinez sans face, and the psycho that was Rebecca Hall.

And they all wanted a piece of her—no, not a piece, *all*. They wanted every inch of her soul; they wanted to tear it up, chew it, swallow it, shit it out, do whatever the fuck they wanted with it and Chase was having none of it.

"You know how this is going to end, Chase," the nurse continued. "You either take the tab or I'll have to call Barney to come in here."

Chase's frown deepened. Barney was another halfwit, only this one was employed by Grassroots Recovery. Grassroots wasn't a prison—she was free to go if she so chose—but while here, there were certain rules that they had to adhere to. And taking your meds was one of the few that were stringently enforced.

Chase sighed heavily and stared at the pill for a moment longer. Then she brought the plastic cup to her lower lip, tossed it back, and swallowed.

"There? You happy?"

Nurse Whitfield sighed.

"Chase, come on."

Chase opened wide, lifted her tongue, and wagged it.

"You want to strip-search me next?"

The nurse ignored the comment.

"Thank you, Chase. Remember, you've got group in an hour."

Chase clapped her hands together.

"Oh, goody; *sharing*, my favorite time of the day."

***

The second Nurse Whitfield left her dorm, Chase hurried to the sink and put her mouth under the tap. She turned the water to freezing cold and guzzled as much as she could. Then she pulled away and jammed the first and second fingers of her right hand down her throat. Chase gagged and she felt her diaphragm quiver in protest.

But nothing came up.

She repeated this act a second, then a third time, but all this served to do was to fill the sink with the water she'd just swallowed.

On her fourth try, Chase finally regurgitated the tab of methadone into the sink. It didn't clink loudly as expected but instead stuck to the porcelain where it landed. She stared at it for a moment, wondering how something that was supposed to help her heal could be so fucking evil.

Then, worried that the nurse might return, she picked the pill up and wrapped it in a wad of tissue. The first two-dozen or so times that Chase had puked up the tab, she'd just flushed it down the sink. But this was before she'd heard a nasty rumor that the Grassroot sinks and toilets had been specifically designed with a mesh to catch large objects and that the tabs could stay in them for up to a month without dissolving.

Chase thought that this was bullshit and considering that the source was a methhead by the name of Randy DeWitt, she was almost certain that it wasn't true, but she wasn't taking any chances.

The prospect of being force-fed the methadone, either by liquid suspension or injection, if they found out that she was flushing the pills, was just too great of a risk to take.

After looking around and making sure that no one was wandering the halls, Chase turned her attention to the cold-water tap. For the price she paid to be here, Grassroots wasted no money on upgrading their fixtures. The tap was the old-school kind, a simple, inverted metal cup. Chase unscrewed it and turned it upside down. She didn't know how many pills she'd stashed inside both the cold and hot water dials over the last four months, but it was well in the double, and maybe even triple, digits. Chase jammed the newest wad of Kleenex in there and was forced to squish it considerably to make sure it fit. Two more months meant a lot of pills; she was going to have to find another place to stash them.

Chase screwed the cold water tap back on, tested it to make sure that it actually worked, and then looked up at herself in the mirror.

No booze or drugs for four months had done wonders to her complexion, which was now a healthy pink as opposed to a monochrome gray hue.

She almost looked alive.

"Two more months," Chase said to herself in the mirror. "Two more months and I can get out of this place without making a pit stop in a federal penitentiary."

The only problem was, after her time at Grassroots was up, where would she go?

Chapter 2

"NO, DON'T TOUCH THE body," Agent Jeremy Stitts snapped. "Just look. Look with your eyes."

FBI Agent Danny Blue recoiled from the corpse as if it was hot to the touch.

"It's just that it seems so real," Danny said in a strangled tone.

Stitts stepped between the greenhorn and the body.

"That's because it—*she*—is real," he barked.

Danny eyed him curiously.

"But she's dead."

Stitts had to chew his lip to fight back another scathing retort.

Of course, she's fucking dead, you idiot. She was shot in the forehead with a .22.

"Don't touch the body without gloves," Stitts repeated in a patronizing tone.

Stitts himself took a small step backward and tilted his head as he stared at the woman splayed out in the center of the room. The bullet hole in her forehead just above her right eye had been so powerful that part of her skull had collapsed from the impact. Blood and brain matter puddled about her head and soaked her long blond hair.

"On second thought, don't touch the body at all. You've got no business touching the body; you're not a fucking medical examiner, you're not a pathologist, you're not *anything*. Just watch."

Something in Danny's face changed then, and he looked younger than his thirty-three years. *Much* younger. And for a moment, Stitts felt sorry for the man. But when his eyes focused on the dead woman on the floor and knowing that there was a dead six-year-old upstairs, any sympathy he might've been harboring dissolved.

Stitts indicated with a hook of his chin for the local detective to join them by the body, which he promptly did.

"You guys grab the husband yet?" Stitts asked.

The detective, an elderly gentleman with wispy gray hair and a clean-shaven face, shook his head.

"He's at the movies, believe it or not. We're probably going to wait until he comes out to grab him, just in case. We've got a couple guys in the theater to make sure he doesn't try anything, but—"

Stitts shook his head and interrupted.

"Unlikely. Based on the MO here, the only other person he's likely to put the gun to is himself. Which wouldn't be half bad, if you asked me."

The detective nodded.

"Fucking sad, isn't it?"

The comment, coming from a man with such experience, surprised Stitts and for a moment he didn't say anything.

"Yeah, it is," he said at last. "Look, we're done here; we'll just wrap up some paperwork and then head back to Quantico."

Even though he was speaking to the detective, it was Danny who answered.

"That's it? We're done?"

The agent's constant slew of questions was so annoying that Stitts was almost overcome with the urge to punch him. Instead, he sighed and rubbed at his eyes and temples, behind which a headache was starting to build.

"Look, Agent Blue," he started, speaking very slowly. "It's cut and dry—the only reason we were called in is because the bastard took his wife and daughter from Baltimore across state lines to Washington. That's it. Nothing else to do here; nothing but sign off on this and hope that Mother Justice puts this asshole away forever."

"Oh, o-okay," Agent Blue said with a slight stutter.

Stitts started toward the door, but when he opened it and looked back, he was annoyed to see that Danny was still hovering over the woman's body. He strode over to the man, grabbed his arm roughly, and gave it a sharp yank.

"I said we're done here, Agent Blue. Now let's go outside so I can have a fucking smoke."

***

"This isn't… this isn't working," Stitts said, rubbing his temples again. He wanted to say more, to complain about all the rookie partners that he been teamed up with over the past few months but couldn't bring himself to do it. Instead, he pinched the bridge of his nose and sighed.

"If you have something to cry about, go talk to a therapist—go see Dr. Thompson. I'm not a shoulder to cry on, much less a sleeve on which to wipe your snot, Stitts," Director Hampton began. "But if you want to talk about how we can fix this problem, then you need to come to me with some genuine ideas of what you want to do. The truth is, Stitts, the partners that you were so quick to discredit, all four of them, scored very highly on all tests. So, before you go off on a rant about what's wrong with *them*, maybe you should look somewhere else first, if you catch my drift."

Stitts felt his blood pressure start to rise. It wasn't the man's lack of sympathy that angered him—he had expected as much from the director—but that the man's words had some truth to them. Maybe the problem wasn't *them* but *him*.

"You need a break, Stitts? Some time off? A little—"

Stitts's eyes shot up.

"No," he replied quickly. The last thing he wanted right now was time off. Time away from the job meant more time to think, to consider what he'd done, to reflect on how he had betrayed one of the very few people he genuinely cared about.

Stitts stood and was met with a searing pain inside his head. His headaches were back; there was no questioning it now. Before, he had attributed the dull throb to a lack of sleep and maybe dehydration.

But now he knew differently; he was being punished.

"All right," Stitts said softly. "Maybe I will go see the doctor, but that doesn't change the fact that Agent Danny Blue is green as they come. I want a new partner. Someone who has experience. Someone who knows what the hell they're doing."

Chapter 3

"CHASE, IT'S BEEN A while since we've heard from you. Care to share some thoughts?" Dr. Matteo asked with a warm smile.

Chase, surprised that she'd been called upon, glanced up. Dr. Matteo was a thin man and where he lacked hair on top of his head, he made up for with an illustrious mustache. Dr. Matteo was the first person she'd met after Jeremy Stitts had dropped her off at Grassroots, and she found him to be a kind, caring, and gentle man. Good at reading people, Chase also knew that he genuinely wanted to help her.

The problem was, Chase wasn't sure that she was amenable to help. Sure, she'd managed with considerable strife to kick her heroin addiction but exorcising the demons from her past was another issue altogether.

Aside from the doctor, there were four others in the room, all of whom were female: Randy, a meth-head who was present only to avoid doing time for shoplifting; Joelle, who claimed to be twenty-three but who looked fifteen, with alcohol dependency issues; Corey, a successful businesswoman who mixed alcohol and cocaine far too often for her partners to overlook; and perhaps the most intriguing of the lot, Louisa, a plump woman who was the mother of two young children, with schizophrenic tendencies that were exacerbated by the consumption of hallucinogens. What Chase found so interesting about the latter was that Louisa had readily admitted to being abducted for forty-eight hours when she'd been very young.

Like, six or seven years young; *Georgina* young.

As for Chase, she had fabricated a story about herself that kept evolving so rapidly that it was a wonder no one had called her on it. You know, safe spaces and all that. There was simply no way that she was going to talk about her time in the FBI, or before that, about what she'd been through, what she'd seen.

That wouldn't do anyone any good.

Only Dr. Matteo was able to tease some truth out of her, mostly because he was attuned enough to pick up on her tells, to identify when she was lying.

"I'm having trouble sleeping," Chase said. One of the things she'd learned very early on at Grassroots was that *not* speaking was one of the worst options. She'd observed firsthand the badgering that ensued, the subversive glances, the frowns, the sheer disgust aimed at those who refused to share. Normally, none of this bothered Chase. The real problem was that if you didn't speak at one session, you were bound to get asked to do so at the next.

And the next.

And the next after that. Wash, rinse, repeat.

"Is it because of your son?" Dr. Matteo asked softly.

Chase nodded. The most recent iteration of her story was that a car accident, in which both her husband and son had perished in, had pushed her to heroin.

This was close enough to the truth that she could react genuinely, but far enough from reality that she could distance herself from it.

"I just keep seeing his face," Chase said. True to form, Felix's face suddenly appeared in her mind. It had been a long time since she had spoken to either Brad or Felix, which was in part imposed by herself—she didn't want them to see her this way—and also because Chase wasn't sure she could handle the rejection if they refused to speak to her again. The fact was, Chase simply wasn't good for them. She had tried—

Lord knows, she had *tried*, first with the move to New York from Seattle, then to Quantico after that. But her past kept following her and it was hellbent on destroying her future.

It was only a matter of time before it happened all over again.

"He's in the car with acrid smoke billowing about his round face. He's yelling at me—no, not yelling, *screaming*. He's asking Mommy to help him, to save him. He keeps repeating that he doesn't want to die." Chase was surprised when her voice hitched during that last part.

"Guilt is the most common reaction humans have to loss. Be it survivor's guilt, or guilt that we weren't there to help the one we love. But the thing about guilt is that when we acknowledge it as such, it loses some of its power," Dr. Matteo said. This was a common refrain from the man, the idea that we need to acknowledge feelings rather than suppress them. Chase couldn't count the number of times the doctor had reiterated that these feelings don't exist outside of our head and that they are a fabrication of our own making.

It made sense, of course, but this realization didn't seem to impact just how terrible these fabrications made Chase feel.

"I just wish I could switch places with him," Chase said softly, lowering her gaze. "It seems so unfair that I get to live for thirty-five years and counting, while he got less than a decade."

"The Lord works in mysterious ways," Randy said suddenly, and Chase's eyes shot up. She was about to say something, to snap back at the woman, when Dr. Matteo intervened.

"Let's focus on what we know to be real," he said sharply. "Your son was killed in an accident, and while you can live your entire life second-guessing every decision that you made that led up to this event—for instance, I should have done the groceries the day before and then he wouldn't be in the parking lot at that time, or if only I had picked him up ten minutes earlier from school, etc., etc.—these are all rear-looking observations that hold no value or merit. And while I believe that it is valuable to hold onto specific memories, it is *not* useful to look back on what could've or would've happened. Our reality at present *is what actually happened* and that is the only thing that we need to process in order to continue moving forward."

"But the Lord—"

Dr. Matteo's mustache bristled.

"Randy, please. Whether you believe in God or not, the fact that he may or may not have played a role in the events that took place is irrelevant. Again, this is a backward-looking approach. What we need to do is focus solely on the present."

"At present, I would like to punch Randy in the face," Chase blurted.

Randy recoiled as if she had been struck.

"I'm only trying to help," she shot back.

Chase looked to Dr. Matteo then, and while she wasn't one hundred percent certain, she thought she saw a hint of a smile form on the man's lips. But rather than intervene, the doctor turned to Louisa and gave her a gentle nod.

"When I was first taken," the woman began, speaking in her characteristic slow, monotone voice, "all I could think about was how I would live my life if I ever got out of there. And even though I was only gone for forty-eight hours, even over that short a period of time, I grew to understand that my present reality was what really mattered. Not what I should've done to avoid being taken, or what I would do if I got out of there. Living in the moment afforded me the ability to take control of my surroundings. To survive. To escape."

Chase stared at Louisa as she spoke, *really* stared at her. After a few moments, the woman's face grew distorted and Chase was surprised to find that her cheeks had grown moist. She wiped the tears away with the back of her hand.

As she did, her thoughts moved from Felix, who was still very much alive and safe with Brad, to Georgina.

Is that what happened to you, Georgie? Did you think about your future, about what you would do when you finally saw me again? Or did you just accept your reality and give in to the bastard that took you?

Chapter 4

STITTS DIDN'T GO SEE Dr. Thompson. Despite what he'd told Director Hampton, he didn't need to see the doctor. What he *needed* was a fucking partner with some idea of what they were doing.

What he needed, was Chase.

Stitts cupped his hand around a cigarette and lit it. As he walked to his car, he inhaled deeply and relaxed when the warm smoke filled his lungs.

For several minutes, he just sat in the parking lot of the FBI training headquarters with his window down. He continued to sit there even as the clouds rolled in and started to block out some of the bright midday sun. When he was done with his first smoke, he lit another.

As he smoked, his mind began to wander, eventually turning to the day when he'd confronted Chase, as it tended to do lately.

When he had given her an ultimatum: go to prison or go to rehab.

It had taken all of his clout, all of his moderate influence, to convince those who mattered to even consider the latter.

After the mess that Chase had made in Chicago, there were a lot of people who wanted to see her in prison, not the least of whom was Detective Bert Marsh. In fact, despite the agreement that Director Hampton, himself, and an unwitting Chase had come to, it was probably best if she didn't go back to Chicago for a very long time.

Stitts wanted to visit her, of course, but every time he called, Dr. Matteo suggested against it. He said that she was in a fragile state and that seeing him might stir up memories, which, in turn, had the potential to trigger a relapse.

And even though he had saved her from prison, Stitts still couldn't help but wonder what other options might have been available to her, to *them*.

"There is no us," he scolded himself.

After a final drag from his cigarette, he flicked the butt out the window. A recruit happened to pass by his car then. She first stared at the still burning cigarette as if it were enriched plutonium, then offered Stitts a sour look.

Stitts gave her the finger and rolled up his window.

He owed Chase his life. If it hadn't been for her, he would have been murdered at the hands of his once partner Agent Chris Martinez. And while he had done his best to help Chase get her own life back, it still wasn't enough.

"Fuck," he swore. It had been four months since he'd last seen her, four months that had been some of the worst that Stitts could remember.

He was about to take out a third cigarette when the phone at his side buzzed. He didn't recognize the number, but grateful for the distraction, Stitts answered anyway.

"Hello?"

"Hi, is this... is this Jeremy?" a female voice asked.

"Who's this?"

There was a short pause before the woman replied.

"My name is Belinda Torts, and I'm a neighbor of Maria Stitts."

Stitts sat bolt upright in his car seat.

"Is she okay? What's wrong?"

"Well, I'm not sure... It's just that... I was sitting—"

"Is she okay?" Stitts demanded. "Is my mother okay?"

Even before Belinda answered, Stitts started the car and backed out of his parking space.

"She's fine... but..."

Stitts exited the parking lot and then jammed the accelerator as he pulled onto the main road.

"Well, then what the hell is going on? Why're you calling?"

"It's just that, well, she's been acting strange lately and today I saw all these guys coming out of her house. *Taking* things out of her house."

Stitts was flying now, ignoring stop signs and stoplights alike.

"What the hell you talking about? Has she been robbed?"

There was another pause, during which Stitts felt his heart race and adrenaline flood his system. His pupils dilated and he swerved just in time to avoid an old man crossing the road.

"Well, not really."

Stitts was gripping the steering wheel so tightly now that he could feel blisters forming on his palms.

"What are you talking about?" he shouted.

"I'm sorry, this is very—"

"Just tell me *what the fuck is going on!*"

"Your mother... it seems like she is just giving all of her things away. I'm not sure... I mean, I think she might be, you know, confused. And now... oh, dear me... Maria... Maria! Please don't take that off. I think you should come quickly, Jeremy. Your mother... she's getting undressed now. She's in the middle of the street and she's getting *undressed.*"

Chapter 5

"YOU'RE LYING."

Chase raised her eyes from her plate of food and stared at the woman across from her.

"Excuse me?"

Louisa put her tray on the table and took a seat.

"I said, you're lying."

Chase turned her attention back to her food. Only after eating a healthy portion of rice did she bother replying.

"Yeah, I heard what you said. Perhaps some context would be helpful?"

Louisa fell into silence, and when she took a scoop of her own rice and ate it, Chase figured the woman was just having an episode.

Chase shrugged and continued eating her meal. When they were both nearly done—despite the considerably larger portion size, Louisa was a fast eater—the woman across from her spoke again.

"Were you in law enforcement?"

Chase froze.

"A police officer, maybe? No—no, I don't think so; you're too small to be a police officer. I would have pegged you as some sort of analyst, but you rarely use your cell phone or any of the computers here at Grassroots. So, what is it, then?"

Chase squinted at Louisa. Not only was she attentive, but intuitive as well. But it was her pleasant face and friendly demeanor that, despite the charge, disarmed Chase.

"FBI," she blurted. The moment the word exited her mouth, Chase wondered why in the world she had said it.

She glanced around furtively and was relieved to note that no one was within earshot. Except for maybe Randy, but she was deep in conversation with her spoon.

"I'm sorry, I have to go," Chase said quickly, rising from the table. To her surprise, Louisa didn't stand with her; she just continued to sit and finish what was left of her meal.

Unnerved, Chase took her plate to the sink and rested it inside. Then she paused for a moment, trying to catch her breath.

Why did I say that? Why did I tell her that I used to be in the FBI?

This was the first time that she had been truthful in months now—*really* truthful—and it put her on edge. She'd spent four months making up a persona and all it took to cause it all to come crumbling down was a simple question from a friendly, albeit strange, woman.

Chase shook her head and looked over her shoulder. Unsurprisingly, Louisa remained seated, but now she was staring at Chase with the same pleasant expression plastered on her wide face.

Chase gave her plate a quick rinse, put it in the dry rack, and then walked over to Louisa.

"Why did you think I was in law enforcement?" she asked, leaning down.

Louisa shrugged and methodically chewed a mouthful of rice.

Chase nodded.

"Okay, I get it. Sure. Communication… it's a two-way street, right? I'll tell you what, Louisa, if you want to chat, swing by my dorm after you finish your lunch."

***

Chase waited patiently in her dorm room for a good hour before giving up.

Louisa wasn't coming. The strange lady had correctly pegged her as a liar, and then just left the comment to fester.

What right does she have to call me out for being a liar? We're all liars here. If we didn't lie, we wouldn't be in rehab. We lied to our husbands, our children, our friends, our parents… we lied when we said we were going to the store for some groceries, only to come back hours later with bloodshot eyes, fresh track marks, and grocery free.

We're all liars… so what right does Louisa have to call me out on it? And why do I care so much?

For the first time in a long while, Chase's left arm started to itch. It wasn't a strong itch, and she easily resisted the urge. The track marks were still there, of course; they had faded over time and unless you were really looking for them, they would be difficult to notice. But Chase noticed. She noticed every one of the small red dots and attributed each of them to a painful part of her life.

They would be with her forever, she knew. No amount of living in the present, as Dr. Matteo instructed, would eliminate the scars of her past.

As Chase paced back and forth inside her dorm, she could feel her blood pressure and frustration rising.

The only thing was, she really didn't know why.

Grinding her teeth now, Chase continued to pace.

Yes, she'd lied. She'd lied to Felix, to Brad, to Stitts. She'd literally lied to everyone she'd ever cared about.

Just as Chase was about to lose her temper, a voice from behind her drew her attention.

"I guess you're wondering why I called you a liar?" Louisa said with a grin as she stepped into Chase's dorm. "Well, because I lied too."

Chapter 6

"**Mom!**" **Stitts shouted.**

Stitts's mother, clad only in a sheer nightgown, stood in the middle of the road. Her blond hair was a mess, completing the illusion that she'd just awoken. Behind her, Stitts could see the door of her semi-detached open wide.

Maria Stitts turned, and when she saw Jeremy, her face lit up. There was a smudge of lipstick that extended beyond her lips.

"Jeremy!" she exclaimed, throwing her arms wide. "So nice of you to visit."

The nightgown she wore was adorned with several prominent coffee stains on the front and was so loose-fitting that he could see the outline of her breasts beneath. A light breeze rippled up the street and her nightgown rose a little, revealing the inside of varicose-ridden thighs.

Stitts hurried to his mother and when he reached her, he wrapped his arms around her protectively and moved towards the house.

"Mom, what happened? Are you okay?"

"Oh, I'm fine, sweetie. Just wanted to get some fresh air."

Stitts glanced around, noting that while no one as of yet had come out of their homes, many a shutter were spread wide.

"Isn't it a beautiful day, sweetie?" Maria said as Stitts led her up the steps.

"Just peachy," he replied. As he grabbed the door, a tanned woman with short black hair emerged from the adjacent house.

Stitts ushered his mother inside and then hung in the doorway for a moment.

"Belinda?" he asked.

The frightened-looking woman nodded.

"I'm sorry to bother you, but it's just that... I mean... I didn't—"

"Thank you," he replied briskly. Before the woman could ramble on, Stitts hurried inside. "Mom? What's going on? What happened—"

All of Stitts's breath was suddenly sucked from his lungs. The house looked as if it had been robbed: the TV, the one that he had bought his mother for her birthday a few years back, was missing from the mantle, all the dresser drawers were pulled out, and even the fucking VCR—*who in the hell wants a VCR?*—was gone.

In a word, the place looked ransacked.

"What the hell happened?" he gasped.

Maria Stitts took a seat in her leather recliner—that, thankfully, was still there—and then crossed her pale legs. Smirking, she pulled a cigarette out of the side table and lit it.

"Oh, honey, you worry too much. Everything's fine. Some friends came by, said they wanted to borrow some stuff. They said they'd bring it back."

Stitts blinked. For a moment, he considered that this was all part of an elaborate prank. After all, the last time he'd seen his mother over the holidays, she'd been fine. Maybe a little more talkative than he was used to, but otherwise normal.

This, on the other hand, was unequivocally *not* normal.

The lipstick on the cheek, wearing a nightgown in the middle of the street, and the... giving away of her things?

Stitts buried his face in his hands for a moment and massaged his temples. Then he pulled free and lit his own cigarette.

"Mom, you've been robbed," he said at last.

Maria laughed then, a high-pitched titter that Stitts had never heard before.

"Oh, don't be silly. It's just some nice guys I met online; they're borrowing some things for a while."

Stitts ground his teeth.

"Online? Mom... how did you... fuck."

The smile suddenly slid off Maria's face.

"Watch your language, Jeremy."

Stitts's mind was racing, running through every possible scenario that could explain his mother's odd behavior. Did she have a stroke? Was she suffering from rapid onset Alzheimer's? Was she drunk? High?

"Mom?" he asked in a soft voice. "Did you take something?"

"Something? Like—" she wagged a finger. "Like *drugs*? Oh, Jeremy, I don't take drugs. You know that. All I—"

A loud knock interrupted the woman. Stitts rested his cigarette on the ashtray and then made his way to the door.

Thinking that it was Belinda again, he pulled it wide, ready to thank the woman for a second time. Only it wasn't her. Standing on the stoop was a young man with bleach blond hair and acne scars on his cheeks.

Stitts's eyes narrowed.

"Uh, is Maria still around?"

"Who are you?"

The man's lower lip curled.

"Who am I? Who the fuck are you? Maria told me to come by and borrow whatever I want."

Stitts's blood started to boil.

"You fucking robbed her."

"I didn't rob shit. She be givin' stuff away, I told you dat. And your girlfriend be—"

"*Girlfriend?*" Stitts snapped. "That's my mom."

The kid sucked his teeth.

"Yeah, whatever. I just came to pick up a watch."

Stitts's mind was boggled.

"You better get the fuck out of here, right now," he seethed.

In his periphery, he saw the punk's hands ball into fists.

"Yeah, what you gonna—"

Stitts lost it; all the stressors of the past few months, starting with what had happened with Chase, then with her incompetent replacements, and now *this*. Without thinking, he grabbed the kid by the throat with his right hand and squeezed hard. The punk's eyes bulged and he instantly started to strike Stitts's arms with his fists. This didn't last long; he stopped when Stitts pulled his pistol from the holster on the inside of his jacket and pressed it against his pale forehead.

"You stay the fuck away from here, you got that?"

The kid wheezed something that Stitts couldn't make out, not that it would have mattered, anyway. There was nothing that he could say that would stem Stitts's flow of rage.

"You stay the fuck away!" he shouted, pressing the pistol against his forehead.

"Jeremy! What are you doing? Let go of him!"

His mother's voice brought him back to reality, and he released the punk. Stitts had pressed his pistol so hard against his forehead, that it left a circular mark directly in the center.

"You fucking crazy, man. You fucking psycho, you know that?" the boy croaked as he stumbled down the steps.

"Get the fuck out of here and never come back!" Stitts shouted after him.

Chapter 7

"**WHAT DO YOU MEAN,** you lied?" Chase asked.

Louisa stepped into the dorm room and closed the door gently behind her. Then she turned to face Chase.

"You and I are a lot alike, and it's not just because we're both mothers. We've been through something, something very similar, if I daresay."

Chase chewed the inside of her lip, trying to figure out what the hell the woman was talking about without giving any more of her own story away. In the end, it didn't matter; Louisa did the talking.

"I wasn't taken for forty-eight hours, Chase," she began, taking a seat on the small cot across from Chase. "I was gone for two weeks. Thirty years ago, I was walking home from school when a van pulled up beside me and offered me a ride."

A lump in Chase's throat suddenly made it hard to swallow. In fact, the situation was so surreal, that she didn't really believe it. For a moment, a brief but tangible period of time, she thought that she was high, that somehow, she had scored some heroin and had injected it.

When she didn't speak, couldn't speak, Louisa continued.

"The man in the van asked if I wanted a ride. It was so hot out and—"

Chase's voice suddenly returned.

"Shut up," she croaked.

Louisa raised an eyebrow.

"Excuse me?"

Chase aimed a finger directly at the woman's face and strode forward.

"You shut the fuck up. I don't know who told you this, I don't know if it was Dr. Matteo, or Stitts, or someone else, but you stop this right now. I'm warning you."

Louisa's calm demeanor suddenly broke and for a second she looked frightened. But then her gaze grew hard again.

"You need to calm down, Chase. I came to you because I think we have something in common. I think that we can help each other—"

Chase was seeing red now. She knew she was about to lose control, to fly off the handle, but she couldn't help herself. This was a sick, twisted game, one that she had no interest in playing.

"How dare you?" she demanded. "How dare you come into my room and talk this bullshit to me."

Louisa held her hands up defensively.

"It's *not* bullshit, it's the truth. All that other crap that you said about your son dying and I said about being lost fortyeight hours, those were the lies. This is the God damn truth. I was taken by a man in a van, a huge man, and I was held for nearly two weeks before I managed to escape. And you want to know what else? I wasn't alone. There were other girls there too, girls my age. I could've saved them, Chase, but instead I ran. And every single day of my life, I—"

Chase punched the woman. She punched the woman directly in the nose. It was a satisfying blow, although, given her posture above Louisa, it lacked the impact she'd intended. Regardless, there was an audible crack followed by a gush of blood from both nostrils. Louisa flew backward and her head landed on the pillow. She was stunned but recovered quickly and avoided Chase's next punch.

Louisa was the much bigger woman, but she lacked Chase's training. When she went to grab Chase's arm, Chase managed to slip from her grip and punched her in the side.

"How dare you!" she screamed. "How fucking—" Chase stopped yelling when someone grabbed her arm. She turned around, intending to land a blow with her other hand before she realized that it was Nurse Whitfield.

"Chase! Stop it!"

Chase looked from Louisa with her bloodied nose and rage-filled eyes, to Nurse Whitfield who looked genuinely terrified.

More shouts and footsteps echoed down the hall, and Chase knew what was going to happen next. She'd seen it once before when Randy had gone off the deep end and smashed her TV. They'd given her an injection of some sort that put her to sleep for the better part of twenty-four hours.

The last thing that Chase wanted to do, no matter how much anger and hatred she harbored toward Louisa at that moment, was to sleep and dream.

She let go of Louisa's arm and stepped back.

"I was trying to help you," Louisa exclaimed, her voice considerably more nasal now that her nose had been broken. "I thought we could help each other."

Chase, still seething, pointed a finger at her forehead.

"You can't help me."

"Calm down," Nurse Whitfield ordered. "Everyone, just calm down. Louisa, make a stop at the nursing station and then head back to your room. Chase, you sit down and regain control of yourself."

Two large orderlies suddenly appeared in the doorway of Chase's dorm with Dr. Matteo in tow. Chase's eyes flicked to the large syringe clutched in one of the orderly's hands.

"What's going on here?" Dr. Matteo demanded.

Louisa's and Chase's eyes met. Louisa looked away first.

"Nothing," Louisa snapped. "I instigated it."

Dr. Matteo gave her a once-over as she walked by, his expression slack. When the woman was gone, Chase felt her blood pressure return to normal.

"Chase, are you okay?" Dr. Matteo asked.

The only thing Chase could do was offer a weak nod.

"I don't know what the hell just happened, but I'll get to the bottom of it. But first, you've got visitors."

Chase recoiled.

"Visitors? I don't think—"

"I don't think it's a good idea either," Dr. Matteo said, lips pursed. "But I *thought* we were making progress."

Chase ignored the comment.

"Is it Stitts? Is it Jeremy?"

Dr. Matteo shook his head slowly.

"No," he said. "It's two people who are supposed to be dead."

Chapter 8

STITTS'S HANDS WERE SHAKING so badly that he could barely bring the cigarette to his lips without fumbling with it.

He couldn't help but think he'd let his mother down. The first thing he had done after the altercation at the door was call his father. After briefly explaining the symptoms, the lipstick, the confusion, his father's diagnosis had been immediate.

"Your mother's had a stroke."

With tears in his eyes, Stitts watched as his mother was loaded onto the gurney by the paramedics and then slid into the back of the ambulance. He wanted to be in there with her, of course, but they wouldn't allow it. Instead, he followed in his own car, smoking cigarette after cigarette, wondering how he'd lost his cool. Sure, he was under a lot of stress, but to put a gun to a kid's head? He was beginning to think that Director Hampton was right, that he needed to see the doctor again.

The ambulance arrived at the hospital less than ten minutes later and Stitts parked out front. He followed the paramedics inside and realized that they must have given his mother a sedative, as she was now calm and relaxed and smiling up at him from the gurney.

His father had been right, of course; his father was always right. After a CT scan, the neurologist confirmed that his mother had had a stroke.

"Is she going to be okay?" Stitts asked with a tremor in his voice.

The neurologist, a beefy fellow who smelled of onions, took a deep breath before answering.

"It's difficult to tell so soon. She's had an ischemic stroke due to a blood clot. We have her on blood thinners and they seem to be breaking up the clot. So far, we don't think that surgery is going to be necessary. We'll know more over the next forty-eight hours. Right now, she's sedated to keep her blood pressure low."

Stitts took all of this in before replying.

"Is it possible that she was suffering from symptoms earlier? For a week or more?"

The doctor nodded.

"It's possible—we don't know exactly how long the clot has been present, whether it started as a partial that increased in size over time. Have you been noticing strange behavior, has your mother been acting out of character recently?"

Stitts felt a pang of guilt in the center of his chest.

"It's been a while since I've seen her," he admitted. "But over the holidays, she was fine."

The doctor pulled out a notepad and started scribbling.

"So, at Easter, you say that she was fine? Completely lucid?"

The pang of guilt became a culpable embrace.

Stitts shook his head.

"No, not Easter; Christmas. I saw her last Christmas and she was fine. More talkative than usual, but she was okay. Made sense. There was none of this..." he let his sentence trail off.

The doctor nodded again, scratched out his previous note, and made a new one.

"Can I see her now?"

"You can see her, but like I said, she's sedated and is unlikely to respond. I'd like to keep her that way for the next forty-eight hours or so. You're welcome to come and go as you please, but we've got your number and will call you if her status changes. Is there anyone else that we should contact?"

Stitts thought about this for a moment before shaking his head.

"No, there's no one else."

***

Stitts was grateful that somebody, probably one of the nurses, had cleaned the lipstick off the side of his mother's face. She looked much paler now than she had back at the house, and with the tubes running into her arms, she looked sick, as well.

No, not sick. If it weren't for the bumping and the beeping of the ECG and other various machines, Stitts thought she looked dead.

"Mom?" he said softly. "Mom, I don't know if you can hear me, but I just wanted to say I'm sorry. I'm sorry for not visiting like I should've. I'm sorry for everything."

He held his mother's frail hand as he spoke, expecting her to squeeze his fingers. It was foolish given what the neurologist had just said, but he still hoped she would respond in some way. That she would open her eyes and tell him that it was indeed okay, that she understood, that he had a very important job to do. That he had to stop the bad people out there.

But Maria Stitts did nothing.

Tears spilled down Jeremy's cheeks and he wiped them away with his fingers. As he did, he was startled by his phone buzzing in his pocket.

He took it out and when he saw that the number was unlisted, he sniffed and wiped his eyes again. Stitts cleared his throat and answered it.

"Stitts here," he said.

"Stitts, Director Hampton. I need you to come in."

A nurse suddenly entered the room and was startled by his appearance. When she saw that he was on his cell phone, she shook her head sternly and indicated with a pen that he should leave the room. Stitts gave his mother's hand a final squeeze and stood.

"Stitts? You there?"

Once in the hallway, Stitts turned back and stared at his mother's flaccid face through the glass partition.

"Yeah, it's me. I'm here."

"I've got another case for you—I need you on this one."

Stitts dried his cheeks with his sleeve.

"Give me fifteen minutes and I'll be there."

Chapter 9

"THEY'RE... HERE?"

Dr. Matteo nodded.

"I find it curious that your dead husband and son managed to fly in from New York on such short notice," he said, no humor in his voice.

Chase ignored the comment—she couldn't believe it. The last time she'd spoken to Brad and Felix... well, she couldn't remember exactly when. She thought it was back when she was chasing after Frank Carruthers in Chicago, but it could have just as easily been before that.

As it stood, she wasn't sure whether she should be happy or furious.

"A word of advice, Chase?" the doctor said.

Chase was barely paying attention now. She had to get ready. She had to clean herself up, brush her hair, put on a little makeup. Look presentable.

"It's going to be difficult to keep an even keel. Remember lessons about living in the present. You should be very pleased that they're here to see you, but irrespective of what they say or do, don't think about what happens after they leave. Enjoy the time with them. Enjoy the moment."

Dr. Matteo continued to speak, but Chase was no longer listening. She walked over to the mirror and tucked her hair behind her ears, noting that it had grown much longer than she was used to, and as a result had become quite unruly. She slapped a bit of water in it to keep it down, but it just sprung back up as soon she let it go. This reminded her of Stitts and his medium-length brown hair that never seemed to be out of place. No matter what the man did, it always seemed to look the exact same.

It's not about Stitts. It's about Felix—Felix and Brad. Stick with the program, Chase.

Moderately satisfied with her appearance, Chase turned back to Dr. Matteo.

"Did they say… did they say why they're here?"

She racked her brain, trying to think of whether or not it was someone's birthday, or an anniversary, or… something. But her mind was so scrambled with excitement and trepidation that she couldn't even remember exactly what day it was. She knew for certain that it wasn't Felix's birthday, but Brad's? Could it be his birthday?

"Chase? Are you going to be okay?" Dr. Matteo asked.

"I… I don't know," Chase replied honestly.

***

Grassroots Recovery wasn't a prison. Instead, it was a voluntary program with one main goal: to reintegrate addicts back into society. Patients were entitled to come and go as they pleased, but if you failed to complete the treatment, there were often consequences.

And in Chase Adams's case, if she didn't keep it together for six months, her consequences might very well be a prison sentence for breaking a fugitive out of a Chicago PD holding cell.

Chase reminded herself of this several times as she waited in the designated visitor space. The room was cozy, complete with couches and a center table, as well as an orderly who continually rearranged a puzzle in the corner of the room. Chase sat down on one of the couches and smoothed her skirt. It was wrinkled, and for some reason of all the amenities that

Grassroots had, they seemed to lack an iron. Five minutes after entering the room, Dr. Matteo opened the door.

Behind him, Chase saw her son.

Felix looked older than she remembered, even though she'd seen him less than a year ago.

When Dr. Matteo stepped out of the way, Chase couldn't help herself. She leaped to her feet and ran at the boy with such speed that the doctor barely managed to avoid being bowled over.

Felix was so startled that he nearly toppled when she squeezed him.

"Felix! Felix, I missed you so much," Chase said, kissing him on the cheeks and forehead. The boy tried to pull away and when he did, she spotted Brad stepping into the room.

They exchanged a look, and Chase turned her attention back to her son.

"Thank you for coming," she said, squeezing him so tightly that he groaned. "I've missed you so much."

Chapter 10

STITTS FLICKED HIS CIGARETTE butt out the window and after rubbing crust from the inner corners of his eyes, stepped out of the car.

He took a deep breath, made sure that his gun was tucked carefully away in his holster, and strode toward the FBI training facility.

Once inside, he didn't bother slowing when he passed his colleagues; he simply walked straight for Director Hampton's office.

He tried to put what happened to his mother out of his mind, but it was a next to impossible task. The only way he would be able to get his mind off things, he knew, was to work.

And to work, he needed a partner.

Stitts took a deep breath and knocked twice on the director's door. He opened it without waiting for an answer.

Director Hampton sat behind the desk, his small eyes looking out at Jeremy from behind round spectacles.

"Did you see the head doctor?" Hampton asked.

"I had a brief session with him after I left your office this morning," Stitts lied. Hampton observed him for a few moments, clearly waiting for him to crack, but Stitts held his ground.

Eventually, the man nodded and then handed a folder over to him.

"A colleague in the Las Vegas Metropolitan Police Department asked for help on a specific case. Last night someone raided a high-stakes private poker game in Las Vegas, killing eleven. Sgt. Theodore thinks that at least twelve million dollars were stolen."

Stitts didn't open the folder as he was prone to do when Director Hampton debriefed him.

Las Vegas… poker… everything was coming full circle.

"You okay, Stitts? I told you that if you want a shoulder to cry on, you're going—"

"I'm not doing this alone," Stitts said bluntly.

Hampton leaned back in his chair.

"You know me, and you know that it's my priority never to send an Agent onto a case alone, especially one of this magnitude. We need someone who has our back out there in the field, someone we can trust. Don't forget that it wasn't too long ago that I was in the field."

Stitts hadn't forgotten; Director Hampton was one of the most decorated FBI Field Agents in the history of the Bureau before transitioning into management. No one knows exactly why he got out of the field, especially considering his success. Some think that after a while death takes a toll on a person, and when you toe the line between life and death for too long, you inevitably end up on the wrong side.

"You said it; I need someone I can trust. Someone who has my back, not some greenhorn who doesn't know his ass from a hand grenade."

Stitts didn't think he had ever spoken so bluntly to the director, but the fact was, he had had enough of this bullshit.

He was going to take the case, that much was clear. Not just because he was obligated to do so from a professional standpoint, but also to take his mind off things.

"I need someone that I have a history with."

Director Hampton's eyes narrowed as he clued into what Stitts was really saying.

"I can't do it," he said simply.

Stitts tossed the folder on the desk.

"Then I can't do that."

Hampton sighed and removed his glasses and laid them on the desk. Then he leaned forward in his chair.

"Agent Stitts, do I need to remind you what it means to reject an assignment?"

"No; there's no need to remind me."

As he spoke, Stitts took his badge and gun out of his pocket and holster and laid them on the desk beside the folder.

They were at an impasse, and for several long seconds, neither man said anything. When Director Hampton found the need to voice his opinion first, Stitts knew that he had the upper hand. But it was more than that; he also had leverage. While he hadn't explicitly mentioned it, Stitts knew things about the director, about Agent Martinez, about a good number of things that would cast an unfavorable glow on the FBI as a whole.

"All this, for her? Are you sure you want to do this, Stitts?"

Stitts remained silent.

"Okay, go get her then. But I'll tell you this once, *just once*, Agent Stitts. If she fucks up again, it's not just her ass on the line. I will personally make sure that both of you go to prison for what happened in Chicago. Do you understand?"

Chapter 11

AFTER CHASE GOT OVER her initial shock of the surprise visit, things calmed down considerably. And when they did, reality set in.

There was something about the way her son looked at her, as if he didn't even know who she was. They talked idly for some time, but in the back of her mind, Chase kept thinking about why they were really here, what this visit was really all about. And that frightened her. As a result, she found herself rambling with Felix, talking about this and that even though the boy was clearly uncomfortable.

All the while, Brad just stood in the background like a wallflower, passively observing.

"And school's going well, sweetie?" Chase asked.

Felix rolled his eyes.

"Mom, you already asked me that. School's fine."

Chase wasn't sure that she had but shrugged anyway.

"Well, forgive me for being interested," she said. She'd meant it as a joke, but when Felix's expression soured, Chase instantly regretted it.

"I'm going to miss it," Felix said unexpectedly. "I like my school."

"Well, that's good to hear, it's always—wait, you're going to miss it? Why are you going to miss it?"

For the first time since they'd arrived, Brad took center stage. He laid a gentle hand on Felix's shoulder and cast a quick glance over at Dr. Matteo.

With that look, Chase knew that at least part of this meeting had been prearranged. Dr. Matteo might have pretended as if he didn't know that Felix and Brad were alive, but it was clear that the two had chatted beforehand.

And this angered her; it was all Chase could do to keep her feelings buried deep down.

"Felix, you think you can spend a little bit of time with Dr. Matteo? I'm sure he has some really cool things that he can show you."

Dr. Matteo nodded and gestured for Felix to come with him.

"Not a problem; I can show you a stethoscope. A stethoscope can be used to listen to your own heartbeat, did you know that?"

As soon as the door clicked closed behind them, Chase scowled.

"Drop the charade, Brad. Are you going to tell me why you're really here?"

Brad sighed and ran a hand through his hair before answering.

"I hate to do this to you, Chase. I really do."

Chase felt her headache returning with renewed fervor.

"Brad, please. Just get to the point."

"We're moving, Chase."

"Moving?"

Brad nodded.

"I got transferred. Look, I never wanted to do this to you. In fact, the last thing I want to do is to take Felix away from you. You *know* this. The only thing I want is for you to get well so that you can become part of his life again."

She shook her head.

"Where are you moving to? I'm here in Virginia and you're in New York. What could be further than that?"

"Sweden," Brad said quickly.

Chase gawked.

"*Sweden*? What the fuck, Brad? You can't be serious."

"I'm sorry, Chase. I just don't have much of a choice. And when you're better, I swear when you're better, we'll work something out."

Chase suddenly felt like punching Brad in the face as she had Louisa not ten minutes prior.

"What do you mean *you have no choice*? That's bullshit—of course, you have a choice."

"What I mean, is that they've transferred me. And I need the money. You're not working now, and—"

Chase rose to her feet and hovered over Brad who was still seated on the couch. He leaned away from her, and out of the corner of her eye, Chase saw the orderly start to creep toward them, apparently dusting the air.

"I have money, you know that. I have more than enough money to support us both… all three of us."

Brad clenched his jaw.

"What money? The money you won from quasi-illegal online poker? Look, Chase, I just want you to get better. That's it. Besides, it's not like you see much of Felix now, anyway."

"What the fuck? I've been here! I've been in this place *trying* to get better so that I can be a better person, a better mother, a better—" she stopped herself before saying *wife*.

Brad's expression softened.

"I know, I know. And that's what I want, Chase. Come on, you know me, you know I don't want to take him away from you. It's just for a little while, anyway."

"A little while? How long is a little while?"

"I don't know for sure; a year, maybe two. Three tops."

And that was it; Chase lost it.

She leaped at her ex-husband then, her hands held in front of her like the claws of a feral cat. Brad was taken by surprise and barely managed to get his hands up in time to protect himself.

The orderly, however, had anticipated this outburst and intervened before Chase could do anything but grab his shirt. The man was strong and easily pulled her back.

"What the fuck, Chase?" Brad said, standing and smoothing his shirt.

"You can't take him," Chase shouted. She redoubled her efforts to try to get to Brad then, but the orderly wrapped his thick arms around her waist and held fast.

Brad slowly started to make his way toward the door.

"You need to get well, Chase. You need to get yourself well and then we can talk about seeing Felix again. I'll leave the number and everything you need to reach him, but please, get well first. He's been through a lot and he's fragile. He misses his mommy, sure, but you don't want him to see you like this."

Brad moved to the door and pulled it wide.

Dr. Matteo stood not ten feet from the entrance, his arm resting on Felix's shoulder. The boy looked at her then, and she saw incredible sadness in his eyes.

"You can't take him," Chase whispered.

Brad walked over to Felix and his arm quickly replaced Dr. Matteo's on the boy's shoulder. And then, without even giving her a chance to say goodbye, he turned her son around and started to walk away.

"You can't take him!" Chase screamed. She tried to squirm loose again, but her efforts were useless. "No, you can't take him! Georgie! Georgie, don't go with him! Run, Georgie, run! Scream and run, Georgie! Don't get in the van!"

Chapter 12

"I'M FINE," CHASE SPAT as the orderly thrust her back into her dorm.

The orderly, who hadn't said anything during the entire ordeal, continued to remain silent. But the man's face, his round and pink and somehow offensive face, said it all: *You're not fine, and if you continue to not be fine, I'll give you the same sedative that I gave Randy.*

Still seething, her blood boiling, and yet not seeing a way out of this that didn't end up with her being in an induced coma, Chase threw her hands in the air.

"Give me some god damn privacy, would you?"

The orderly gave her another look, but eventually acquiesced to her request and left her alone in the room.

Only after the door was firmly closed did Chase allow her emotions to overwhelm her. Only it wasn't rage or frustration anymore, or even fear. Now it was only one solitary emotion that polluted her soul: guilt.

Chase's guilt manifested as body-racking sobs and tears that fell like Niagara Falls.

"Fuck," she muttered in a slobbery mess.

She went to the mirror and stared at her reflection. She looked like a completely different person than earlier in the day.

"Fuck," she repeated.

Everything I touch, everybody I've ever cared about, suffers.

Without thinking, Chase found herself unscrewing the top to the cold-water tap. She flipped it over and stared at the pills wadded up in toilet paper and buried inside.

Her fingers worked on their own accord now, unpacking the pills and putting them on her tongue. She swallowed the first one dryly, as well as the next two. The fourth was considerably more difficult and the fifth made her gag. Chase ended up spitting this pill back into her palm and then had to turn on the hot water to slurp it down.

The sixth pill hadn't made it to her lips before there was a knock at the door.

Chase wiped her face with the back of her arm, and for the briefest of moments, she thought that it was Brad coming back, coming to tell her that he had changed his mind. That he was going to take her out of this godforsaken place and bring her home so that they could be a family once more.

But her family had been taken from her long before she had ever met Brad, or even thought about having a child of her own.

Chase squeezed the pill tightly in her palm and opened the door.

It wasn't Brad; in fact, it was the last person she expected.

It was Louisa, complete with gauze stuffed into each nostril and eyes that had already started to darken with a bruise.

"Look, I'm sorry about what happened, Chase, but—"

The woman stopped abruptly, her eyes skipping to Chase's own, to the sink which was still running, to her clenched fist.

"What the fuck are you doing?" the woman demanded. Chase was still furious at Louisa, but her reaction was so strange that she took a step backward.

This sealed her fate.

The woman rushed at her, taking Chase by surprise. Before she knew what was happening, Louisa had her pushed up against the sink. Her fingers were pried open next, and the tablet fell into the basin and then down the drain.

"No," Chase tried to say, not because she was losing the pill—she still had plenty of those—but because for some reason she was inexplicably worried that Dr. Matteo, or maybe even Nurse Whitfield, would find it.

This made no sense, of course, given what she had already consumed.

But the word barely made it out of her mouth, on account of the fact that Louisa's fingers were on their way in. Bent over at the waist, the porcelain sink cutting into her hips, Chase vomited.

At first, it was only the water she'd consumed with the last pill that came up, but as Louisa's fingers scraped along the roof of her mouth, and then throttled her uvula, up came the pills.

As she retched, Chase realized that Louisa was saying something, that she was saying the same thing over and over and over again.

"You don't want to do this, you don't want to do this, you don't want to do this."

When Chase, through blurred vision noticed that there were six pills in the sink, she bucked her hips, knocking Louisa backward.

Then she whipped around and stared at the woman, no longer filled with rage, but with something else.

The woman had just saved her life. Why, Chase had no clue.

"I came to tell you that you have a visitor," Louisa said.

Chase was confused. Did she mean Felix and Brad? Did she mean the meeting that they'd already had?

As if reading her mind, Louisa shook her head.

"No, a uniform type—someone like you."

Chase's confusion only deepened

"A unif—"

And then she saw him. He looked tired, but his medium-length brown hair was perfectly coiffed, just as she remembered.

Chase blinked several times, and then wiped her eyes. The tears were gone, but the mirage remained.

She opened her mouth to say something, but for the second time in as many minutes, Louisa gripped her shoulders and pulled her close.

"When this is over, whatever *this* is, we need to talk. Like I said before, we have something in common. A *lot*. And I think I can help you."

"What?" Chase asked. But Louisa had already let her go and was moving towards the door. The woman nodded at the man as he approached Chase's dorm, and he returned the gesture.

Then he entered.

The two of them locked eyes for a moment, neither saying a word. And then Chase broke; she stepped forward and embraced him. He, in turn, wrapped his arms around her, gave her a quick squeeze, and then released.

"Chase, we need you back," FBI Agent Jeremy Stitts said. "*I* need you back."

PART II – Restitution

THIRTY-SIX HOURS AGO

Chapter 13

CHASE INHALED SHARPLY.

It had been a good four or five months since she'd seen a dead body, and a long time before that since she'd seen so many in one place, if ever.

The room was large, but so far as Chase could tell, it wasn't of the typical variety designed for sleeping. For one, there were no beds to speak of; in fact, aside from the overturned poker table and ergonomic chairs, and what appeared to be a semi-permanent bar erected in one corner, there was no furniture at all. The room was a simple square that was drenched in blood.

The crimson liquid soaked the green felt of the poker table and speckled all four walls. An expensive bottle of tequila had been smashed at the neck and lay on its side atop the bar. Tequila slowly dripped from the bottle's jagged opening and, mixing with the blood on the bar, made for a slow pink drip that seemed almost hypnotic as it fell to the floor and soaked the carpet.

"Eleven victims," Stitts reminded her, and Chase turned away from the bottle. "Seven players, the dealer, bartender, and two security guards."

Chase nodded and made her way deeper into the room; despite going over the preliminary file multiple times on the plane, and then again in the car on the way from the airport to The Emerald Hotel and Casino, she tried to see the scene with a fresh set of eyes.

The bartender was lying on his back behind the bar, his face so covered in blood and riddled with bullet holes that it was unrecognizable. He was lying on his back, his arms out at his sides, shattered bottles all around him. The poker players were scattered around the toppled table like dolls. The dealer was located closest to where he sat during the game, his body more or less wedged in the groove cut from the table. He was sitting cross-legged, which Chase thought odd, and his head was slumped all the way forward to the floor, which caused his back to arch unnaturally.

There was a single bullet hole in the back of his head.

Chase walked slowly around the carnage, careful to avoid most of the blood splatter that the hazmat-clad CSI members were either in the process of photographing or sampling. As she moved, Chase tried to piece together the order of events that had led to such carnage, her eyes moving first to the door from where she'd come in, to the security guards next. The two men, large, muscular fellows dressed in black suits, lay toward the back of the room near a row of thick, yellow-tinted windows. Chase indicated the security detail with her chin, both of whom had been shot multiple times both in the chest and neck and face.

Stitts followed her over to them, and Chase knelt next to the larger of the two men, who was collapsed on his side.

"What is it?" Stitts asked. This was his refrain, of course; to ask questions and to wait for answers. Not to make assumptions or assertions even if he already knew the answer.

"The door's over there," Chase said, pointing back the way they had come in. "There's no other entrance or exit to this room."

Despite its odd phrasing, she'd meant the comment as a statement and not a question, and Stitts saw it as such.

"So why are they over here if they're supposed to be guarding the money and players? Wouldn't it make more sense for them to stand closer to the door?"

Stitts nodded and called for one of the CSI techs. A man with slicked black hair sporting a white plastic suit hurried over to them.

The man stared at Chase for a moment.

"Yes, Agent Adams?" the tech asked.

Chase's brow furrowed; she hadn't announced her presence or introduced herself to anyone but the Sgt. who had led them to the room.

Keep it together, Chase. He probably just recognized you from one of the many stupid things that you've done in the past.

She pushed these thoughts from her mind and pointed at the man's left hand, which still clutched a semiautomatic 9mm pistol.

"Can you tell if his gun has been fired?"

The CSI tech removed a swab from a pouch on his hip, and he wiped the barrel of the gun with it. A second later, he showed it to her.

It was dark from GSR.

"Check to see if the other guy fired his gun," Chase instructed.

Although there were bullet holes everywhere—high-power rounds embedded in the walls and the victims—there was only one in particular that she was looking for.

As her eyes drifted around the room, Chase was consciously aware that Stitts was staring at her.

Let him stare, she thought.

She was used to people staring at her, watching as she twitched and shook then vomited on herself, all the while begging for her next fix.

Chase bit the inside of her cheek again, drawing her back to the present.

"Where are you…" she whispered. "Where are you?"

And then, just as her eyes started to grow tired, she found it: the bullet from the security detail's gun. Only it was in one of the last places Chase expected.

Instead of near the door, which would make sense given that that was the only direction from which the assailant or assailants could have entered the room, Chase found the bullet embedded in the ceiling *behind* her.

She pointed at the small crater near where the wall of windows met the ceiling, and Stitts's brow furled.

"Why would… you think he was falling maybe, squeezed off a round as he was going down?" Stitts asked after a pause.

Chase thought about this for a moment before shaking her head. It didn't make sense. In a game of this magnitude, with ten or more million dollars on the line, all of which appeared to have gone missing, The Emerald wouldn't use rent-a-cops. They'd hire highly trained security.

Chase rose to her feet and made her way over to the bartender once more.

Of all the victims, it appeared that this one was either the target or had somehow raised the ire of the killer.

As she hovered over the poor man's body, the room darkened, and the rustling of the CSI techs, the dictation by some forensic pathologist on the scene, and even her own breathing seemed to go quiet.

Chase squatted by the bartender's outstretched arm and noticed that his hands were a mess—the fingers on both hands ragged from shattered glass.

But she had no interest in his hands.

Chase took a deep, shuddering breath and reached for him. A split-second before she made contact, Stitts's palm came down on her shoulder.

"Are you sure you're up for this?" he asked in a quiet voice.

Chase looked over at her partner. His face was slack and his eyes wide.

The man cared... he cared too much.

Chase took another deep breath and nodded.

"Ready as I'll ever be," she said out of the corner of her mouth.

And then she touched the corpse's bare skin.

Chapter 14

SHOCK CROSSED OVER CHASE'S features.

Nothing happened.

Swallowing hard, she gripped the man's cold flesh a little tighter. In her periphery, she saw Stitts lean forward, and she closed her eyes as if she were seeing a vision. Before, back in Alaska, and then Boston and Chicago, all she had to do was touch the corpses, and Chase was ushered away to another world, her mind reconstructing the scenario that led to their murder. It wasn't clairvoyance or voodoo as Stitts liked to joke, but a reconstruction of the evidence that her subconscious picked up on, but that Chase wasn't aware of.

Only not this time; this time, nothing happened.

Chase moved her fingers a little, trying to ensure that she had enough skin to skin contact.

And then she tried to picture the man holding the bottle of tequila, smiling, getting ready to pour a drink when the door exploded inward and the bullets started flying.

Only in her mind, the vision Chase created seemed like a cartoon or an over-the-top action film and not reality.

"It doesn't look like the other security guard fired his weapon."

Chase opened her eyes and nodded at the tech.

Then she turned to Stitts and, not sure what else to do, gave him a curt nod as well.

Trying to hide her confusion, she rose to her feet and stretched her back.

"We need backgrounds and histories on everybody here — everyone from the dealer, to the players, to the security guards," Chase said.

Stitts stared at her curiously for a moment before replying.

"LVMPD's already on it. You okay?"

Chase shrugged.

"One more time," she whispered for her own benefit as much as Stitts's.

She squatted and pulled the man's shirt sleeve up a little, revealing a sparrow tattoo on the inside of his forearm.

It'll work this time, it's just taking some time because you're out of practice.

Chase reached out with both hands this time and gripped the man's pale arm as if she were preparing to give him an Indian sunburn. The palm of her right hand covered the sparrow tattoo, and it briefly registered in her mind that it was prickly to the touch. And then she squeezed; she squeezed *hard*.

But there was still no vision.

Chase didn't hear the clink of bottles as the bartender arranged them prior to the players arriving, nor did she hear the explosion of assault rifle fire, moments before his face was caved in by the ammunition.

She heard, and saw, nothing.

Uttering a curse under her breath, Chase let go of the man and rose to her feet. Then she turned to look at Stitts, who had concern in his wide eyes.

"You sure you're okay?"

Chase shrugged her partner off.

"Fine," she grumbled. And then, to no one in particular, she said, "We're not going to find any trace evidence here. These guys were pros."

With that, Chase strode from the room, hoping that Stitts was following.

From the outside, she appeared calm; on the inside, it was a different story. Chase's heart was racing in her chest and her mind was abuzz.

What happened to me? Why can't I see?

Chapter 15

HER HEAD SPINNING, CHASE made her way into the hallway and leaned her back up against the wall. The entire seventh floor had been cordoned off and was full of uniformed officers and techs milling about.

Somehow, despite the chaos, Chase managed to block out the noise and was in the process of regulating her breathing, when she was interrupted by Stitts.

"You okay, Chase? You seem—"

Chase waved him away.

"I'm fine," she said for what felt like the hundredth time. "Jesus Christ, do you have to keep asking me that?"

"Alright then, what did you see?" Stitts asked, his face hardening.

The order of her partner's questions—first asking how she was, and then what she had seen—reinforced Chase's notion that Stitts really did care about her.

"First, I need to clear my head," she said. "I need to go for a walk."

With that, she pushed herself away from the wall, flashed her ID to the officer manning the elevator and stepped inside.

"Hey, wait up," Stitts said, hurrying after her.

But Chase didn't wait up.

"Lobby," she said quickly to the officer. The man nodded and pressed the *L* button.

"Chase? Hold the elevator," Stitts said.

Without hesitating, Chase reached out and pressed the close button.

The doors closed in front of Stitts, a confused expression on his face.

There was no better place in the United States of America, and perhaps the world, where you could lose yourself as fully and completely as you could in Las Vegas. In fact, that was exactly the point of Las Vegas; to forget about everything. Nothing about it was real. The hotels were fake, made to look like something else—Paris, the Stratosphere, New York, New York, they didn't even bother pretending to be original or unique. They only had one goal: to transport the visitor to whatever world they wanted. For a weekend, for an hour, for a day, you could be ultrarich, you could be important, you could leave your boring, mundane life at home and be anyone, anywhere.

Which suited Chase just fine.

As she entered the lobby, Chase was immediately inundated by the chimes and beeps and whirrs and buzzers of the slot machines that filled nearly every square inch of The Emerald.

Under other circumstances, Chase might've been amused by the facade that was Las Vegas, but not now.

Not after what she'd seen upstairs. Not after the bartender's face had been obliterated by bullets.

Chase walked briskly, her head low. The amazing thing about Las Vegas was its ability to continue in the face of… well, pretty much anything. When the shooter in Mandalay Bay had taken out hundreds of people at the Route 66 concert below, the hotel never even shut down—not completely, anyway. Even now, with nearly a dozen bodies lying upstairs and millions of dollars stolen, nobody down in the lobby seemed any the wiser.

And this facet posed a particular problem when it came to crime. Sure, Vegas was known for having more cameras per capita than any other place in the world—and Stitts had informed her that the LVMPD was going over the footage not only in the casino, but in the surrounding casinos, parking lots, everywhere they had eyes—but when it came to witnesses? No one tended to see anything. People were in their own worlds, transported by Las Vegas itself.

Chase walked by a woman who looked to be in her mid-eighties, sporting a pair of sweatpants with an unsightly bulge from the diaper beneath. It would've been comical had it not been so sad. She watched as the woman tapped a few buttons on the slot machine, and the wheels started to spin.

And this is what it has come to, she thought. *Why bother pulling the handle when you can just push buttons and play as fast and furiously as one could?*

So many icons filled the screen, that Chase didn't think it humanly possible to actually follow what was going on. Several lines lit up, and the digital coin total on the corner of the screen started to increase.

But you couldn't tell that the woman had won by looking at her. Eyes glazed over, the octogenarian brought her Virginia Slim to her mouth and took a puff. When the chiming ended, she hammered some more buttons and the wheel started to spin again.

There was something undeniably sad about this, but something also very familiar to Chase.

In life, it didn't matter how much you made, how much you lost, how old you lived to; there was just one or two things that really mattered, things that you kept returning to. And for Chase, there was only one thing that still held meaning.

She was partway to the front doors of the casino when a commotion behind her drew her attention.

Several officers started rushing toward her, their faces grim. Some were barking loudly into walkie-talkies, which was nearly sufficient to knock Virginia Slim from her trance. Her attention locked on the woman at the slot machine, Chase was nearly bowled over by a man wearing a wide-brimmed khaki-colored hat.

"What's going on?" she demanded. When no one even acknowledged her, let alone stopped, Chase grabbed the arm of the closest officer and flashed her FBI badge.

"What the hell is happening?"

The man, a young cop with green eyes and a square jaw, stared at her for a moment before finally answering.

"There's been an explosion," he said under his breath. "Someone's bombed the Planned Parenthood clinic just around the corner."

Chapter 16

CHASE WAS SURPRISED TO see that the sun had started to peek over the horizon. Inside the casinos, time was like Schrödinger's cat: unless you specifically looked at a clock or watch, you really didn't have any clue what time it was.

As the officers hurried to squad cars filling The Emerald's circular drive, Chase went the other way, toward Stitts's rental. Halfway there, however, she realized that not only was Stitts not at her side, but that she didn't have the car keys, either.

Chase swore under her breath and glanced around.

Where are you, Stitts?

A hand suddenly came down on her shoulder and she spun around.

"Thanks for leaving me at the elevator," Stitts said sharply.

"Sorry," Chase grumbled. "Needed to clear my head."

Her partner gave her a look as they walked toward his rental.

"Looks like there was a bomb at the Planned Parenthood clinic over on Essex," Stitts said as he opened the driver-side door and slid inside. Chase nodded as she got into the passenger seat.

"That's what one of the officers told me—anything else to go on? Fatalities? Damage?"

Stitts shook his head and put the car into drive, pulling in behind the line of squad cars.

"Don't know yet. The explosion was small, but other than that, details are scarce."

Chase nodded again and stared out at the skyline as the sun continued to rise.

As Stitts drove away from the strip, the casino skyline gradually flattened. Soon, the glitz and glamor started to wane and was slowly replaced by a brown smudge. Outside of the strip, and perhaps Old Vegas, poverty and crime were much more prevalent. But none of the forty plus million annual visitors wanted to see that, not in a world of their creation. For the most part, it was the authorities' job to keep these facts from the public eye.

A fire truck blocked access to Essex Ave, but a glut of police cars stopped them long before that. In the distance, Chase could see tendrils of smoke licking the horizon, battling the early morning sun.

Chase and Stitts exited the vehicle and joined the throng of police officers observing the scene. Stitts led the way, holding his badge out in front of him for anybody who wanted to take a quick peek. As they neared the fire truck barricade, a man who looked as if he was in charge, a man with a thick mustache and a shaved head that was mostly covered by a khaki colored hat, stepped forward.

His dark eyes flicked from Stitts to Chase, then to Stitts's badge.

"FBI Special Agent Stitts," the man said with a nod. "We didn't get a chance to meet before, but Director Hampton said that you were on your way."

He held a hand out and Stitts shook it.

"This is FBI Special Agent Adams," Stitts said, and Chase shook the man's hand next.

"Sgt. Steve Theodore," he offered in return. "I was heading up the investigation at the casino when I got called out here. Looks like we have an improvised explosive device that went off outside a Planned Parenthood clinic. So far, no casualties and damage is limited."

Chase peeked around the man's shoulder as he spoke, trying to take in the scene. Someone sporting a thick, green bomb suit moved down the street, following closely behind a bomb-disposal robot.

"Bomb squad is clearing the scene now, but it will be at least another hour before we can get in there and better assess the damage."

"Any idea on motive?" Stitts asked.

The Sheriff chewed the inside of his lip and tilted his head to one side.

"It's a Planned Parenthood clinic…" he said, letting his sentence trail off.

An officer appeared at Sgt. Theodore's shoulder and whispered something in his ear. Theodore nodded.

"Listen, I need to go deal with the press right now. And I'm going to be honest with you, the bombing is likely going to be a top priority moving forward."

Chase scoffed and the Sgt. shot her a look.

It made little sense to her that a bomb in which no one was injured took precedence over eleven dead and twelve million missing dollars, but she should have expected as much. If the target had been a Walmart or Whole Foods, no one would give a shit. But Planned Parenthood? That took top priority; it was just the political climate in which they all were forced to endure.

"I'll give you guys all the support you need," the Sgt. continued, "but you're going to have to head up the investigation at The Emerald on your own. There's a free office across the hall from mine back at the station, if you want it. Now, if you'll excuse me, I've gotta go feed the rats."

The man didn't wait for a response; he simply nodded, turned, and left.

"Feed the rats," Chase murmured under her breath. She'd never heard that expression in reference to the press before, but rather liked it.

Stitts nodded and pulled out a cigarette.

"Cool new habit you've got there," Chase said. The remark was ridiculous coming from her, given her past, and in particular, the incident at Grassroots moments before Stitts arrived, but she was unable to control herself.

Tyler Tisdale used to smoke like a fiend during their time together, and the second hand always reminded her of him, of a time she desperately wanted to forget.

"Stress," he replied, taking a drag. "Anyways, we better get going. We've got a lot of work to do."

Chapter 17

CHASE COULDN'T REMEMBER THE last time she'd been to a police station that was so empty. Located just off the strip, the station was nearly deserted. There was a secretary out front, someone to flash their badges to, but other than that, there was nobody. If it hadn't been for Stitts and his keen eye noticing the placard outside of Sgt. Theodore's office, they never would have found the empty office across the hall.

The door was unlocked and inside they found two desks facing each other, a whiteboard on one wall and a push board on the other. There was also an archaic computer on one of the desks, but Stitts pushed this aside in favor of his laptop, which he immediately opened and started typing away at.

Chase, curious as to what her partner was doing, dropped her bag on the free chair and headed over to him.

She was surprised to find that Stitts was IMing with someone back in Quantico about the bombing.

"Need to see if there's chatter about the bombing on any of the alt-right channels," he offered, his tone defensive.

Chase shrugged; she knew that Director Hampton, like Sgt. Theodore, would be all over this, as well.

She didn't like it, but there was nothing she could do about it, either.

Live in the moment, Dr. Matteo's voice echoed in her head.

That was difficult to do, given that Chase's mind was continually drawn back to the scene at the casino, and what *hadn't* happened.

After touching the girls in Alaska, and then in Boston and Chicago, her visions had left her feeling nauseous.

But now... now that she seemed to have lost the touch, or whatever the hell it was, Chase felt downright terrible.

What's worse, was that self-doubt had begun to creep in like a dark cloud.

If I can't use my skills... if I can't trust my gut anymore, then what good am I? How will I ever find her?

Chase pinched the bridge of her nose and collapsed into her chair.

Along with self-doubt, something else started to nag at her.

Back in Alaska when Chase had first experienced one of her visions, she'd been drinking. In Chicago, she'd been straight-out using heroin. But now, ever since she'd gotten clean—

No, she scolded herself. *That can't be it. You're better now. You're better, you're healthier, you're smarter.*

But even as these words formulated in her mind, she quickly dismissed them. They sounded fake.

They sounded like some cheesy PSA special.

There was a knock at the door, which startled Chase, and she let out a small gasp. Noticing that Stitts was staring at her, Chase felt her face redden.

How long has he been looking at me like that? she wondered.

The man in the doorway was in his mid-sixties, with gray hair that clung to his temples and deep grooves around his nose and mouth. In one hand he held several folders, while the other was gripping a wooden cane that looked to be supporting most of his frame. With every step, he grimaced.

"I assume you guys are the FBI agents?" he asked in a surprisingly young-sounding voice, given his appearance.

Stitts quickly got to his feet and relieved the man of having to walk all the way over to him for an introduction.

"Special Agent Jeremy Stitts," he said, before hooking a thumb over his shoulder. "And this is Special Agent Chase Adams."

The man offered a thin smile.

"Greg Ivory," he replied. The lack of a mention of rank—be it Officer, Detective, Sgt., Sheriff, Deputy or whatever the hell they had here in Nevada and Las Vegas—struck Chase as odd. "Sgt. Theodore told me to convene with you guys. I have all of the information we've gathered thus far on the security, the bartender, dealer, and some of the players that were at the game last night."

Stitts took the stack of folders from Greg's hand and opened the first one.

"He also told me to help out any way I can," Greg continued. He cast a wistful glance down at his leg and cane. "I won't be chasing any perps anytime soon, but I know my way around, and I have connections. Anything you guys need, just let me know and I'll lend a hand."

"Thanks, Greg," Stitts said, making his way back towards his desk.

Greg turned to leave, but before he did, Chase spoke up.

"Have the families been informed yet?"

The man turned and stared at her for a moment before answering.

"Sgt. Theodore had two officers out doing that before the bomb incident. So far, they've informed the mother of the bartender and three of the players. The company that was outsourced for security was also notified."

Chase raised an eyebrow at this last part.

"Outsourced?"

She'd assumed that the two dead security guards were hotel staff.

Greg nodded.

"The company's called Luther's Investments. It's common for outside help to be contracted for high-roller private games.

More efficient that way," he hesitate. "And generally safer, too. Companies like Luther's Investments have a bunch of ex-military men with good track records on call."

Chase's mind flicked back to the single shot fired by security that was embedded in the ceiling.

Ex-military...

She chewed the inside of her lip and watched as Stitts spread images from the files across his desk.

"Information about Luther's Investments is in their file. LVMPD has even used them from time to time for support on large events."

Chase mulled this over.

If Luther's Investments used legit ex-military as Greg suggested, and not Army Medics but actual Marines or Frogmen, then what are the chances they would get only a single shot off?

It was starting to look more and more like an inside job.

"Anything else I can be of assistance with?" Greg asked from the office doorway.

"Yeah," Chase said hesitantly. "I need a list of anybody who stepped foot on the seventh floor of The Emerald in a forty-eight-hour window flanking the time of the shooting. I'm talking maître d', housecleaning, any waiters that might've brought up food, window cleaners, guests, etc. Anyone at all; if they were there, I want a file on them. And video. I want any and all video from The Emerald and the surrounding casinos on the strip."

The man grimaced, a subtle gesture that would've otherwise been overlooked had Chase not been paying such close attention.

She got the impression that Greg wasn't used to his current role, not yet, anyway. And that, combined with the pain so clearly etched on his face every time he shifted his weight, suggested that his injuries were fresh.

It appeared as if I might not be the only one dealing with changes, Chase thought glumly.

Eventually, Greg nodded.

"I'm just down the hall," he said. "And just a heads-up: it's going to get crowded in here with what happened at Planned Parenthood. Holler if you need me."

Chapter 18

"**Does this make any** sense to you? Any sense at all?" Chase asked, staring down at the photographs of the two men that Luther's Investments had provided for security. The first was an ex-Army Ranger by the name of Terry Ames. The other man, while he wasn't ex-military, was equally as qualified: Tony Peacock spent four years as a SWAT member in Detroit before moving to Las Vegas for what he likely suspected would be a cushy job.

As Chase stared at Tony's photograph, her mind superimposed an image of his face from the hotel room, blood coating his thick beard.

You must've thought this was going to be an easy job. That you would get away from the grind of Detroit and come to the bright lights of Las Vegas to protect some paranoid millennials with too much money and not enough sense.

"What do you mean?" Stitts asked.

Chase gave him a look.

The man knew exactly what she meant, he just wanted her to verbalize it. Normally, this would annoy Chase, but given the fact that her other talent had failed them, the least she could do was to humor him.

"Ex-SWAT and ex-Army Ranger taken by surprise, only one of whom fires a single shot at the ceiling no less? The way I see it, either the men who robbed the game were hyper-trained or it was an inside job."

"Diminishing returns," Stitts said quietly.

Chase raised an eyebrow.

"Say what?"

Stitts started rooting through the photographs and notes that were spread across his desk. For some reason, the clutter made Chase anxious, and she scooped up a handful of photos and walked over to the board with them. After sticking them up with the available pins, she said, "Do continue, oh wise master."

Stitts chuckled.

"Well, how big is the hotel room?"

"Not sure," Chase replied.

"Twenty-two foot by eighteen foot."

"Your point?"

"Well, you have an ex-SWAT member and an ex-Army Ranger in a confined space where a shootout takes place. Even if Ninjas stormed the room, you'd think that security would be able to get off more than one shot. Not to mention, the killers didn't leave a single piece of trace evidence behind."

As Stitts spoke, Chase turned her attention to the images on the board. The man was right of course. Put two or three or maybe even a half-dozen men with guns in confined spaces and training beyond a certain point didn't matter so much. Bullets were going to fly and people were going to get shot.

It was possible, however unlikely, that the men from Luther's Investments were taken by surprise, but with only one way in and out of the room? If surprise was a factor, it would have to come from *within* the room itself.

"And that brings us full circle," Chase said. "There had to be an inside man."

She walked over to Stitts's desk and stared down at the scattered photographs, not of the crime scene—Chase had already put those on the board—but of the victims from the files that Greg had provided.

"When did you get so damn messy," she muttered under her breath.

"Since my parents got divorced when I was nine," Stitts offered. Chase, unsure of whether or not he was joking, looked at him and shook her head. Then she collected all of the headshots and put them across the top of the board, above the respective images of their corpses.

"Well, if it was an inside job, then someone got fucked," Chase said as she scanned the horrific images of the massacre. "*Royally* fucked."

Chapter 19

WHEREAS SEVERAL HOURS AGO Chase had never seen a police station so empty, the opposite was true when ten o'clock struck. She was in the process of going over the details of each of the victims, the many detailed reports of their activities leading up to the poker game, when a portly man wearing an oversized suit that looked like it was straight out of a Dick Tracy movie knocked on the door.

"Can I help you?" Chase asked.

The man's eyes darted around like a frog's searching for the last fly on earth.

"I think you're in my office," he said.

Stitts, who had been punching away at his computer since early dawn, finally looked up and unplugged his earphones.

"I'm sorry? Who are you?"

The man strode forward, imbued with a sense of purpose and self-confidence, and held out his hand. He shook Stitts's before turning to Chase.

"Josh Haskell, DoD. Sgt. Theodore told me I could use this office."

Before Stitts could answer, a second man entered the room, this one even larger than the first, his burgeoning belly so huge that Chase felt sorry for his belt.

"Duane Gwynne," the man offered without being prompted. "ATF. I'm supposed to use this office."

Chase watched the two men in the doorway shake hands before turning to face them.

"FBI Special Agent Jeremy Stitts and this is Special Agent Chase Adams," Stitts offered. "Sgt. Theodore said we can use this office for the investigation. We're more than happy to share, and as you can see on the board behind us we already have some details about the victims. We also have—"

"Victims?" Duane barked, his thick, dark eyebrows rising up his forehead. "There were no victims."

"That's right," Josh Haskell replied. "No victims have been identified as of yet."

A look of confusion crossed over Stitts's face and Chase could literally hear the gears inside his head turning. She stared at the two men in the doorway and then turned to look at the photographs on the board.

Of course, she thought with a scowl.

"You're not here for the murders, are you?"

Duane shook his head, which set the wattle beneath his chin into perpetual motion.

"No, we're—"

Chase didn't let the man finish.

"This office is going to be used for the investigation of the eleven murders at The Emerald, not for a fucking pipe bomb that was set off by accident."

Duane's eyes narrowed.

"Listen, Ms. Adams," he began.

Chase felt a whole mouthful of man speak coming her way and aimed to stem this nonsense before it started.

"No, you listen, Mr. Duane. We were given this office by Sgt. Theodore and it will be used to investigate The Emerald massacre."

Now it was Josh Haskell's turn to get his back up.

"The FBI has no jurisdiction over DoD," he said.

"Nor ATF," Duane offered with a smug expression.

Chase nodded and pushed her lips together slightly, mocking them both without them even realizing it.

"Oh, thank you so much for *edumacating* me. I mean, I'm just new at this. I'm just a little girl and I don't know much about anything."

Stitts, true to his nature, acted as a peacemaker before things got out of hand.

"I get it, we're on different cases with different priorities. But we can share the space. I'll sit over there with you, Chase, and you two…"

It was clear by the expressions on all their faces that this was not going to be a solution that would work. Even logistically, what Stitts was proposing would prove problematic.

Chase couldn't imagine these two walking heart attacks sharing a desk.

The headache behind her eyes that had been threatening to mature pulsed and Chase pinched the bridge of her nose to stave it off.

If it hadn't been six months since her last fix, the last time she'd used, Chase might have thought this was a withdrawal headache. But it couldn't be… not now. Could it?

"Yeah, I, um," Duane started, speaking so slowly that it was nearly painful. "I just don't think that's going to work. We have a politically charged bombing that has terrorist implications here, people. So far as I see it, it takes precedence over the shooting of some ultrarich gambling addicts."

The callousness of the man's words struck a chord with Chase, which was likely his intention, and she lashed out.

"Oh, I get it. Because they were rich, they don't—"

And then, as if this were a Monty Python sketch, a new man poked his head into the room.

Unlike the first two, this one was slim and gaunt, with arms so long that Chase couldn't see him putting his hands in his pockets without them folding at right angles.

"What's the problem here?" the man asked with an air of authority.

Chase suddenly felt like she was back in high school; someone had yanked on Becky's ponytail and everyone was blaming each other.

Her head started to pound.

"The feds think they got this room to *theyselves*," Duane offered. "For that shooting up at the casino over there. They says that Sgt. Theodore gave it to them."

The man looked at Chase, then Stitts, and then managed somehow to squeeze his way between Josh Haskell and Duane Gwynne.

"Well," the man said. "This isn't Sgt. Theodore's office to give. This is an LVMPD station and he's part of Nevada DPS—we only loan him the office across the hall." He shrugged. "You guys are going to have to learn to share."

Chase, grinding her teeth against her headache, stood and started toward the door.

"I'll tell you what, you guys all take your dicks out, line 'em up, and see which is bigger," she looked directly at Duane when she spoke. "If you can find the damn things. Then, when you're all done jerking each other off, please tell me where I can sit so I can do my fucking job."

The men were so shocked by her words, that they nearly toppled as she squeezed by them and into the hallway.

Chase hurried toward the station entrance, once again desperate for fresh air. Behind her, she heard Stitts apologizing and telling the other men that he'd be right back.

Chapter 20

"WELL, I'M GLAD TO see that the time off hasn't changed you completely," Stitts said in a tone that Chase found difficult to interpret.

It appeared that her ability to sense what people were feeling or thinking extended beyond the dead and had now crossed over to the living.

Chase stared at her coffee cup for a few moments while she fought the urge to apologize.

"It's ridiculous; we have eleven dead, Stitts. And they've got a fucking pipe bomb outside of a Planned Parenthood building where no one was even injured. You know, if this bomb was placed anywhere else, aside from maybe a church or mosque, then we wouldn't be having this discussion. In fact, I don't even know if it would make the news. But as it stands, I bet it's running 24/7 right now—our case won't even make an appearance until after the first halfhour."

Stitts sipped his coffee and took his time before answering.

"So what?" he said at last.

Chase raised an eyebrow.

"So what? So *what*? It's fucking bullshit, that's so what, Stitts."

The waitress came by and asked them if they'd decided on their order. Chase said she'd stick with the coffee, while Stitts ordered himself a bagel with cream cheese and lox.

"Not hungry?"

Chase shook her head.

"Lost my appetite."

When the waitress left, Stitts picked up where he'd left off.

"This might be a good thing, something that we can use to our advantage. You know, with all the other cases—" he cleared his throat and corrected himself. "With the *last* case, it was all we could do to keep the media at bay. But with *this* case, with all the news coverage focused on the bombing, maybe we can work undercover for a while."

Undercover, Chase thought, her mind turning to her time, albeit brief, that she'd spent undercover in Chicago.

Stitts must have also realized his poor choice of words, as he quickly continued.

"We won't have to waste our time with the media or be bogged down by any of that bullshit. Look at it this way, what if a bomb had been used in The Emerald hotel room instead of automatic fire? Then we'd be playing second fiddle to the DoD, ATF, bomb squad, you name it. Everyone would be jamming their fat fingers in the pie, squishing it *aaalll* around."

Chase cringed at the analogy but understood what her partner was saying. He could have left it at that, but he was just getting warmed up. The man interlaced his fingers and leaned forward, his eyes peering into hers.

"You ever heard of the Pizza Bomber? Of Brian Wells?"

Both the name and the moniker sounded familiar, but Chase couldn't quite place it.

"Well, it's a long story that revolves around a man—Brian Wells—who robbed a bank with a bomb around his chest. Only thing is, he claimed that he was forced to do it on the threat of detonation. He ended up with a hole in his chest, and it wasn't until years later that the entire thing was figured out. Apparently, Brian had been in on the plot the whole time under the pretense that the bomb was fake. But he was double-crossed and, needless to say, the bomb was very real."

The story came flooding back to Chase, including how Brian's family rejected the court's ruling that he was in any way involved in the plot. They claim to this day that he was just a victim. It was a real clusterfuck of a case, and yet Chase didn't see the connection.

"Anyways, I worked on that case—first year out of the Academy, I was. And I saw firsthand how fucked up things got when the ATF, DoD, Grandma Jones, Uncle Phil, and Geraldo got involved. Look, my only point is that we're better off without the involvement of the other agencies. I have faith in you and I have faith in me to get this thing solved. Who gives a shit if we have to share an office with Wilford Brimley and his type II diabetes? You need to let that stuff go, Chase."

Chase's headache suddenly bloomed.

Live in the moment, Chase.

She sipped her coffee.

Fuck you, Dr. Matteo. In several 'moments,' my husband and son will be halfway across the world and a killer will still be on the loose in Las Vegas.

"Yeah, I guess," she concluded.

The waitress returned with Stitts's brunch, and he ate in silence for several minutes before addressing the elephant in the diner.

"So? You going to tell me what you saw back at the hotel? Share your voodoo? Because we could really use some insight into this one, Chase."

Chapter 21

"A GIRL'S GOTTA HAVE some secrets, doesn't she?"

Stitts swallowed a hunk of bagel smothered in cream cheese.

"Seriously?"

"Let's just go over what we know first before we come to that," Chase said with a smile.

Despite her outward appearance, on the inside, Chase felt only one thing: shame.

At least back when she'd been hopped up on drugs and alcohol, she'd brought something to this partnership. Her strange 'touch' had provided insight that had directly led to solving several cases.

But now that her ability to read the crime scene had apparently vanished, what could she offer? What could a fucked-up ex-heroin addict with a temper problem who is recently estranged from her husband and son provide in this case?

For the second time that day, it dawned on Chase that the loss of her ability coincided with her giving up booze and drugs. It wasn't unreasonable to think the compounds had heightened her sense somehow, and if only—

Chase shook her head.

No. Just no, Chase.

"You okay?" Stitts asked.

"Yeah, fine. Just tired," she lied. "I'm not used to big city lights, if you know what I mean. More into saunas and yoga."

Stitts smirked. There was no way he was buying that Chase had spent more than two minutes in a yoga class before throwing her hands up, uttering a curse, and walking out.

Chase wondered briefly what Stitts had done to get her reinstated. The last time, he had either hidden or changed both her psych eval and medical results. And that was *before* what she'd done in Chicago.

She couldn't imagine what hoops Stitts had to go through this time. And yet, that wasn't what needled Chase most.

That luxury was afforded to the *why*.

Staring at the man across from her, Chase wondered why in the hell he would go out on a limb for her, especially given the way she'd treated him over the past year or so.

The lies, the deception, the downright illegal activities she always seemed to get them both wrapped up in.

Again, Chase shook her head in an attempt to clear her thoughts.

"You almost done? I need some fresh air."

Stitts wiped his hands on his napkin and then tossed it onto his plate.

"All done," he said, rising to his feet. He put a ten on the table and then led the way to the door.

Once outside, he immediately lit up a cigarette.

"I said fresh air, Stitts."

Stitts exhaled a thin stream of smoke on the side opposite Chase, and she took this opportunity to stare at him for a moment. Despite being the one who claimed to be tired, it was Stitts who was wearing the fatigue on his face like an ill-fitting mask. He had dark circles under his eyes and looked like he hadn't shaved in several days. Chase had been so caught up in her own issues that she hadn't even bothered checking in with him, despite already having spent the better part of a day together.

"Are you... are *you* okay, Stitts?"

Stitts was in the process of bringing the cigarette to his lips when she asked the question, and Chase noted a slight hesitation.

"Fine," he lied.

Chase opened her mouth to say more, but then shut it again. When she was *'fine,'* it was because she wanted to change the subject. But this wasn't her... this was Stitts. The same Stitts who had been open about his emotions going way back to the day they'd met in NYC.

And yet, for some reason, Chase found herself unable to probe deeper.

He took another drag.

"So, where do we go from here, Chase? We've got no evidence, no suspects, and a murderer that somehow managed to transport in and out of a hotel room. I mean, this is Vegas, but Houdini died a long time ago."

Chase sighed. Their feelings would have to wait.

"I sent out feelers to some of my poker buddies online," she began. "A lot of the guys that I know from there play live games, too. Not usually at the same blistering stakes, but high-stakes nonetheless. Only two of them knew about the game — one of whom was invited, an online player who goes by the screen name 'ATM,' while I think the other just heard about what happened afterward. But that's only of the people *I* know; it's clear that even though these games are supposed to be secret, people know about them. I also raised a flag out there saying I was interested in the next game, if there is one, to see if any funky replies filter in. Unlikely, but if the killer or killers are online players too, you never know."

"You think it might be personal?"

The obliterated face of the bartender flashed in Chase's mind and she shuddered.

"Not with the players, I don't think. But I wouldn't rule it out in general," she replied.

"All right, sounds good. Greg's compiling information about anyone who stepped foot on that floor around the time of the murders, and we should be getting access to the casino video feeds soon," Stitts added.

"What's his deal, anyway?"

Stitts turned to look at her.

"Who?"

"Greg. There's something about him that seems off."

Stitts rocked his head side to side as he thought about this.

"I dunno," he said after a pause. "He doesn't seem to be liked much by his peers, that's for sure. But he's the only person who's helping us at all, so please don't ask him to take his dick out and measure it."

Chase chuckled, picturing the horrified expression on Duane Gwynne's fat face.

"You can't win a pissing contest without taking your pecker out, Stitts."

They continued walking down the strip, Stitts smoking cigarette after cigarette, Chase observing the throngs of people.

They passed a husband and wife who were swinging their five-year-old daughter between their arms. The girl was squealing with glee, while the parents had deep scowls etched on their faces.

Probably blew her college funds at the craps table, Chase thought. *Who would bring a child to Vegas for a vacation, anyway? Who in the fuck would take their son to live in Sweden?*

Chase swallowed hard.

"What about the wives, sons and daughters, families of the players who died?" she asked. "They might've known about the game. We should also look into the backers."

Stitts raised an eyebrow.

"Backers?"

Chase nodded.

"It's rare for pros to go into these high-stake games using their own cash. Usually, they hedge their bets, pardon the pun, which means they get a bunch of rich friends or colleagues to put up a significant portion of the buy-in. Then, depending on the outcome, they split the profits."

"Really? I thought some of these guys were super rich—like eight or nine figures rich. I mean, I didn't recognize any of the victims from TV, but still."

"Yeah, but the TV guys are just that: TV guys. They can play, sure, but most of the time they already made their money, and the stuff they do on TV is just to increase their Instagram followers. More face time, literally. But the guys who play in these big games, like the one in The Emerald? They're real business people. It makes no sense to put all your money on the line, especially when there are dozens of people vying for the opportunity to do it for you. In any event, I assume that at least half of the seven players had backers. These things obviously aren't public, but the information could be found out if you knew where to look. And they would most definitely know about the game. Perhaps not the details of where it was being held, but at the very least how much was at stake and a general idea of when the game is going to take place."

Stitts turned his face away then, his gaze drawn by the roller-coaster that ripped through New York, New York.

"So, we've gone from a private game with eleven people inside, all of whom are killed, to potentially… what? A dozen more that knew about it? And that doesn't include hotel staff or guests. Looks like the investigation just got more complicated."

Chase couldn't help but think of what Stitts had said about how difficult it had been to coordinate with the ATF, DoD, and state and local PD; he was probably right about being better off without them. After all, now that backers were likely involved, Stitts had no idea how complicated it was about to get.

After all, poker players were in the same league as the best liars in the world—their wealth depended on it.

And Chase considered herself one of them.

Chapter 22

Eventually, when the lights of Vegas were dangerously close to becoming permanent fixtures on their retinas, Chase and Stitts made their way back to the station. And if they had considered it a madhouse before, it was a veritable insane asylum now. Chase could barely get in the door even after flashing her credentials. Apparently, not only did the F in FBI come after ATF and DoD in the alphabet, it also followed them in hierarchy as well.

After name-dropping Sgt. Theodore and purposefully *not* mentioning Greg Ivory, they were reluctantly granted access. They were met with further resistance when they arrived at "their" office, but eventually, they entered that, too. Duane Gwynne was at Stitts's desk, while Josh Haskell had taken up residence at Chase's. Such nice guys that they were, they had neatly piled Chase's belongings and placed them on the floor beside the waste bin. They had also been courteous enough to remove the photographs that Chase had neatly arranged on the pegboard and had layered them on top of one another so that only the face of the bartender remained visible.

Neither man raised their eyes as they entered, and Chase looked to Stitts for advice on what to do next. She was seething, of course, and desperately wanted to tell these men to go fuck themselves. While F might come after A and D, it didn't stand for Federal Bureau of Investigation as much as it did Fucking Bitch Incarnate at that very moment.

Stitts lowered a calming hand on her shoulder and she felt some of her misplaced anger start to dissipate.

"Gentlemen," Stitts said in a friendly tone.

Both men looked up and Chase felt her blood pressure rise when a grin, not a shit-eating grin so much as a diarrhea smear, appeared on Duane Gwynne's fat face.

"You guys back?" Josh asked. "I piled your stuff up there, tried to be all neat about it, to keep it the way it was."

This time, Chase couldn't control herself.

"Gee, thanks. So kind of you."

Josh's brow furled.

"Wait, you mean that you're not… you haven't been… you're still in this office? I thought that with the media coverage of the bombing, that you would be—" he shrugged—"relocated."

Duane chuckled, or he had a minor infarct—it was difficult to tell which—and Stitts's grip tightened on her shoulder.

"No, we're—"

Somebody suddenly appeared behind Chase and she whipped around, reactively taking a defensive posture.

She relaxed when she saw it was Greg and was genuinely surprised that the man had managed to sneak up on her given his noisy cane and ambulatory difficulties.

"What?" Chase snapped. When she saw Greg's face contract inward, she calmed her tone. "What is it?"

"I just wanted to give you the heads-up that the officers completed their rounds."

"Their rounds?"

Greg nodded.

"Yeah, the men met with the families of the deceased. And I think we have a bit of a problem."

Stitts stepped protectively in front of Chase.

"What kind of problem?"

Greg opened his mouth to answer, but before he could speak a shout filtered to them from down the hall.

"Where's his watch?" a female voice shrieked. "Where the hell is his watch?"

Greg hooked a thumb over his shoulder.

"*That* kind of problem," he said.

***

"No, you don't understand—you're not listening. Mike wouldn't go anywhere without his watch."

Chase stared at the woman across from her, focusing on her tear-sodden cheeks, her rheumy eyes, unkempt hair.

"Ms. Hartman, I'm very, very sorry for your loss," Stitts began, leaning across the table.

The woman recoiled as if she'd been struck.

"No, no, no, no, no. You can't do this to me. Everyone else in this fucking building is the same—the police officers, the detectives, *everyone*. *I'm so sorry for your loss*. I'm telling you, like I told them, that my son would never go anywhere without his watch. It was a gift from his father."

Chase watched the woman as she spoke, confirming that her pain was genuine. She also knew from experience that it wasn't uncommon for people who had just lost a loved one to place inordinate value on inanimate objects. It was their way of dealing with the loss, of retaining something to hold onto forever.

"We are working around the clock to find out who did this," Stitts said, the woman's face growing more pinched with every word. "Is there anybody—"

Chase decided to interrupt. She knew that if Stitts continued along these lines they would lose the woman and any valuable information that she might hold.

"Ms. Hartman, do you have a photograph of the watch? Can you describe it to us?"

The woman's face relaxed and she breathed a sigh of relief. Someone was finally listening to her.

As if waiting for this very moment, Ms. Hartman reached into her purse and pulled out a photo and handed it to Chase.

Chase stared at it for several seconds, taking in all the details. The watch was an old timepiece, the kind with a large digital display that was popular in the mid-eighties and early nineties. Dark black with a leather band that was clearly added post-market, it appeared to have little financial value.

"And your son never leaves home without this, is that correct?"

The woman nodded enthusiastically.

"Never."

Chase looked over at Stitts then and took a deep breath. She recalled the way Mike Hartman's face had been caved in by gunfire, and she swallowed hard before asking her next question.

"Ms. Hartman, I need to ask you something, something very important. But it might be upsetting. Would that be alright?"

The woman hesitated, but eventually nodded. She wiped tears away from her eyes with nicotine-stained fingers.

"Did you identify your son's body? Are you sure it was him in the hotel room?"

The woman exploded in waterworks and Stitts hurried to her, handing her a box of tissues and putting a reassuring arm on her back.

For a moment, Chase thought that she had pushed Ms. Hartman too far and that it had been she who had lost her.

"He's my son," she said softly. "You think I wouldn't recognize my own son?"

Son or not, it would've been difficult for anybody to identify Mike Hartman's body in the shape Chase had seen it in the hotel room.

As if reading her mind, the woman cleared her throat and continued.

"He's got a tattoo—a sparrow—on the inside of his right forearm."

Chase nodded.

She'd seen that sparrow, had touched it. Chase had hoped that it would transport her into Mike Hartman's last moments among the living. But in the end, all she got was a handful of cold, dead flesh.

Chapter 23

"No, something just doesn't make sense," Chase said. Ms. Hartman had since been escorted from the building and Greg Ivory had been gracious enough to let them share *his* office. While it was smaller than the one that the ATF and DoD had commandeered, Greg was a thin, tidy man who appeared to be one of the few people who gave a fuck about The Emerald shooting victims.

Stitts had stolen the pegboard and Chase had put it back to the way it was before Duane had rearranged it. Only now, there were more pictures on it, including a series of secondary characters that Greg had unearthed by speaking to hotel management: a waiter who had brought food up to the room during the game, two window cleaners, a maid, and a couple from Montreal who were the only other guests on the floor.

"None of this makes sense," Stitts muttered.

Chase ignored the comment.

"Why would the people responsible for an eight-figure heist care about a shitty Timex watch? Why risk leaving trace evidence?"

Greg shook his head.

"They didn't leave *any* evidence. No trace at all. All fingerprints in that room belonged either to the players or staff."

Chase opened her mouth to say something, but then furrowed her brow.

"Wait—*none*? It's a hotel room. It should have dozens of prints, hair, etc. Shouldn't it?"

Greg rifled through a stack of papers until he found the one that he was looking for.

"The seventh manager, Shane McDuff, said that the room was often reserved for high-stakes games. He also said that it hasn't been used for about six months or so."

Chase chewed the inside of her lip.

"Is it possible that someone was hiding in the room before the game was arranged? Like, days before? In the bathroom or something?"

Greg shook his head.

"I doubt it. I'm guessing that security would have swept the room beforehand. Oh, and it doesn't look like we're going to get anything from the bullets fired. Generic rounds fired from a Colt AR-15."

"*One* AR-15?" Stitts asked, finally chiming in.

Greg nodded.

"So, *one* guy did all this? One guy who mysteriously got in and out of a single-entrance hotel room without being noticed by two highly trained security guards, the staff, or the players?" Chase shook her head and then repeated what Stitts had said moments ago. "None of this makes sense."

Her mind suddenly flicked back to when she'd grabbed the bartender's arm in the hotel room.

Why hadn't I seen anything? Why the fuck in this case, when we've got nothing at all to go on, do I turn out to be useless?

Perhaps sensing her frustration, Greg changed the subject.

"Maybe he just forgot it," the man offered.

"What?"

"The watch," Greg clarified. "Or he could've sold it or lost it. I mean, Mike Hartman didn't live with his mother, and she admitted that she hadn't seen him in at least two months prior to his death."

Stitts suddenly bowed his head and started to type away at his laptop.

"I don't know about that," he said after a few seconds. "Take a look at this."

Chase walked over and waited for Greg to reach her side before Stitts showed them a series of photographs from Mike Hartman's Facebook page.

Most depicted the young, good-looking man living the life as a bartender in Las Vegas. He was poolside, he was in a club, he was riding in a car that was likely a rental, smiling broadly. And in the photographs that showed his arms, the cheap Timex was proudly displayed. Most shots also revealed the sparrow tattoo just above the watch.

"What's the most recent picture?" Greg asked.

"He hasn't posted in about a month," Stitts said, turning back to the keyboard. Eventually, he brought up a photo that was in stark contrast to the others. "This is it."

Mike was staring into the camera, likely the one on his computer, chin resting on his palm. He had dark circles around his eyes and his hair, neatly coiffed in the other photos, was a mess. The caption read, *'Despite what they say, you were a great man. I miss you every day. TRGR.'*

He was wearing his watch.

"I guess that solves that," Greg said. "His mother was right—it doesn't look like he takes the damn thing off."

"What's *TRGR*?" Stitts asked.

"*The Rich Get Richer*," Chase replied absently. "What if... what if this was personal? Like Mike pissed someone off and he was the real target. After all, he looked like he got the worst of it. If I were to rob the game, I'd make sure that I spent most of my bullets on the security and not the unarmed bartender."

Stitts stroked his chin.

"Use a robbery of this magnitude and kill ten other people as a front to off a Las Vegas bartender? One would think there'd be easier and less risky ways of getting the job done. After all, we're surrounded by miles of desert."

"Less profitable, however. Anyways, I was just spitballing," Chase replied.

"Yeah, it might be worth looking into Mike a little more," Stitts agreed. "It's not like we've got anything else to go on here."

Greg nodded.

"When I was in the field, a buddy of mine used to run errands, gather intel for me. I can ask him to do a little digging."

Stitts raised an eyebrow.

"A CI? Why not just get one of the officers to ask some questions?"

Greg's lips twisted.

"They're occupied. Besides, I don't think they would be amenable to requests from me."

Chase waited for the man to elaborate, but when he stayed mum, she turned her eyes to Stitts.

Her partner shrugged.

"No intervention, just observation?" he asked.

Greg nodded.

"Sure. I'll just ask him if he can get a read on the man's character, etc. Find out who this 'good man' is he mentions in his last post."

"Fine. I'll work on getting some more video footage. Still waiting on surrounding casinos, see if anything was pointed near the seventh floor around the time of the shooting."

Chase couldn't help but shake her head in frustration.

"This is Las Vegas for fuck's sake, and the only video we have of that floor is the hallway? Are we absolutely certain that there is no footage from inside the room? No exterior cameras?"

"I'll speak to the manager again, but according to his interview..." Stitts let his sentence trail off.

They'd already seen the video from the hallway: the only person who entered the floor during the game was a waiter who brought food to the room. And he left it at the door.

"Then how the fuck did the person get in and out of the room?" Chase snapped. "The windows?"

"Impossible. They don't open," Greg replied.

"And they were in perfect shape when the police arrived on scene," Stitts offered.

Chase frowned. The windows had also been unblemished when she'd been there, when she'd touched Mike Hartman's arm.

"Can we bring up the video of the hallway again? I mean, is it possible that it was altered in some way? *Mission Impossible* style?" Chase asked.

"Not according to hotel management. All digital video recordings are stored in a highly secure facility, off-site, with extremely limited access. Even if someone managed to mess with one of the recordings, there is literally no way to alter the master. At least, that's what I was told," Greg replied.

Chase felt pressure build in her chest, a manifestation of her frustration.

If only I could see, if only I could see...

"Bring up the video, then," she said to Stitts, trying to distract herself from runaway thoughts.

Her partner nodded and turned back to his computer. As Chase watched him move to the secure case folder, her phone buzzed and her heart skipped a beat.

Is it Brad? Is it Brad, telling me that he changed his mind?

It wasn't Brad.

It was a text message from her poker contact *ATM*.

Stu Barnes was one of the backers, the message read. *He lives in Vegas.*

Without a word to Stitts, who was still searching for the video, Chase hurried over to her computer and searched first Google and then Facebook for the backer.

There were six Stu Barnes living in Vegas, but when she saw the photograph of a silver-haired fox wearing what was clearly a bespoke suit, Chase knew that this was *the* Stu Barnes.

"I have to go out for a bit," she said under her breath. Then she looked up. "Stitts, I have to go—I'll be back in an hour."

Chapter 24

CHASE KNEW THAT STITTS would object; in fact, if the man didn't protest her leaving alone, she would've thought it strange.

"Let me come with you," Stitts pleaded. They were standing in the parking lot of the police station, and her partner was holding the keys to their rental car hostage.

Chase shook her head. She had to meet Stu Barnes and she couldn't do that with Stitts in tow. In fact, she hadn't even decided if she was going to approach him as an FBI Agent or as a grieving poker player. Either way, she would be better off alone; it would be easier to get a read on the man that way.

"You need to trust me, Stitts. We're not going to be able to get anything done if you don't trust me."

The words sounded hollow even to her own ears; how in the hell could Stitts trust her?

Fooled me once…

"I just… I'm worried about you, Chase. Give me a break here."

And there it was again: Stitts wearing his emotions not just on his sleeve, but out in the open air like a foul smell.

Chase sighed and rubbed her temples. The headache that had started earlier in the day had subsided somewhat when she had thrown herself into the case, but it was slowly starting to rear its ugly head again.

And her arm was starting to itch again, too, which was even more disconcerting.

Pulling a page out of Stitts's book, Chase refrained from speaking. Instead, she just held her hand out expectantly.

"Chase, let me come with you," her partner said, even as he handed over the keys.

Chase was defiant.

"I need to do this alone, Stitts. I need to speak to the backer to see if he knows anything about last night. If we show up together, we're not going to get anything. These gamblers—backers or players—they're... well, they're secretive. The only reason I think I can get him to talk is because I speak his language. We've got nothing so far; I don't want to risk blowing it by getting his guard up. How 'bout you speak to the manager, and then we'll meet up again for an early dinner?"

Stitts scowled.

"It sounds like I'm not going to see you until tomorrow."

"Ouch," Chase said, surprised by the way the barb stung. She took a deep breath. "I guess I deserved that, Stitts. And I can't apologize enough for what happened, for what I put you through. I can't even imagine what lengths you went to, to get me on this case. But that doesn't change the fact that there are eleven people dead—eleven people that no one in this goddamn city seems to care about. You need to trust me, Stitts. Trust me, so that I can do my job."

How can you do your job if you can't 'see,' a voice inside her head said. *What good are you without that?*

"Please," Stitts said as he stepped away from the car, "if you need anything, and I mean anything, Chase, just call me. Call me and we'll figure it out together. It just... it just can't be like last time."

The concern, the genuine concern in her partner's voice was so touching that Chase couldn't say anything for fear of her voice cracking. Instead, she simply nodded at her partner and then got into the car.

As she drove away from the police station, Chase hoped that Stitts was wrong.

She hoped that she would be able to overcome the temptations of Las Vegas and return to him before the sun dipped below the horizon.

As a gambler, however, she knew that the odds were not in her favor.

***

Stu Barnes was sixty-three years old and worth somewhere between 150 and 250 million dollars. He initially made his wealth in manufacturing, by teaming up with his father and investing in a plant in China prior to the influx of goods from that country. Shortly after his dad died, Stu made several shrewd investments on his own, with his big windfall coming from Twitter and Uber.

At least, that was what she could find out about the man online.

As Chase pulled up the long winding drive to Stu's mansion near the city limits, she was reminded of a time long ago when she had driven up to a similar house, also with terrible news to offer. Only on that occasion, it had been to tell a woman that her husband had been murdered.

As Chase parked and stared at the large front door of the mansion, she instinctively checked that her badge was still in the inside pocket of her jacket, and that her gun was still in the holster at her hip.

But the longer she sat there, the more Chase started to reconsider her approach. Was it wise to arrive unannounced and interrogate a man who had just lost several million dollars? Not to mention the fact that the player he backed was likely a friend.

A friend who had been murdered less than twenty-four hours ago.

In her mind, Chase constructed two scenarios: one, Stu didn't know of the murders and went into shock or, worse, lashed out when she told him; or two, he knew about them, and his lawyers had already prepped him for what to say to the authorities should they come knocking.

"Fuck it," Chase said, removing her badge and gun and tossing them into the glovebox. If Stu clammed up, they would be back to where they started.

Which was nowhere.

With a deep breath, she stepped out of the car and made her way towards the door.

Chapter 25

JEREMY STITTS WATCHED HIS partner leave in a cloud of exhaust.

What am I doing? What on earth am I doing?

He still couldn't believe that he let Chase go. After all the times she'd lied and taken his car to score dope or to do whatever the hell it was that she did, he let her go *again*.

Oh, don't be silly, Jeremy. She's just borrowing the car, sweetie, his mother's voice chimed inside his head. *She'll bring it back.*

He could still picture his mother's smile, the lipstick extending onto her cheek, her glassy eyes.

"Fuck," he swore. It had been more than twenty-four hours since she'd been admitted, and there was still no word from the hospital. He took his cell phone from his pocket and debated calling to check in on her, but before he did, he shut his eyes for a moment.

This time, it wasn't his mother's face he saw or even Chase's. It was the terrified expression in a young, pimply kid's eyes as Stitts pushed the loaded gun against his forehead.

No, focus on the case. Solve the case, then go see her. If you call her now, you'll only be distracted.

Stitts realized that his free hand had been balled into a fist, and he looked down at it. His nails had dug into his palm so deeply that they left white indentations when he finally relaxed his fingers. They were like the many crescent moons of another world. A world where he wasn't so stupid as to let Chase go off on her own.

Why did I do that?

Instead of calling the hospital, Stitts scrolled to Chase's name instead and his thumb hovered over the call button.

In a way, Chase was right: partners needed to trust each other, their lives could depend on it. But he couldn't trust her; he'd be an idiot to. She was a liar, she was an addict, and she was suffering from untreated PTSD from the loss of her sister all those years ago. Worst of all, Chase was as unpredictable as she was unstable.

With a deep breath, Stitts slipped his phone back into his pocket. Calling her now would do no good. Chase was gone; she had lied and manipulated him again.

And he'd been complicit.

Sweat forming on his brow, generated by equal parts Vegas sun and anxiety, he turned back to the police station. There were more government employees here at present than there were in all of Quantico. And yet, Stitts couldn't help but feel alone.

He made his way back to Greg Ivory's office, where he found the man staring at the images on the board. Stitts did the same.

"What are you thinking?" Greg asked, startling Stitts out of his head.

I was thinking that I should start looking for a new job. Maybe a good lawyer, too.

"I wanna have a chat with the floor manager—with Shane McDuff. Problem is, my partner just borrowed my car."

Greg's eyes remained locked on the board.

"She's got a chip on her shoulder, doesn't she?"

Stitts's initial reaction was to become defensive, but then he realized that Greg was just making an observation and didn't mean to be insulting.

And it was the truth, of course; Chase *did* have a chip on her shoulder.

"She's a complicated woman, that's for sure," he found himself saying, without really thinking. Wishing to change the subject, he added, "Think I can borrow your car? You're welcome to come with, if you want."

Stitts got the sneaking suspicion that Greg didn't like being left alone at the station. Alone among many, like Stitts himself.

"We can take my squad car. But you're driving, my leg aches like hell."

Stitts nodded.

"Not a problem."

***

"How long have you been with the LVMPD, Greg?"

Greg stared out the window as he answered, a clear indication that he wasn't comfortable talking about himself. But, as Stitts knew, the key to trust was being open and vulnerable. And if he couldn't quite trust Chase, then he was going to take his chances with this man who seemed helpful in the face of a bunch of political bureaucrats.

"Thirty-three years last month," he answered. As was his habit, even though Greg paused and appeared to be done speaking, Stitts didn't immediately jump in with another question. Instead, he allowed his first to simmer, to marinate, to give Greg a chance to think about whether or not his answer was satisfactory.

Mostly, Stitts knew that people just wanted to be heard, and you couldn't listen if all you did was ask questions. Eventually, Greg opened up, as Stitts knew he would.

"I started as a beat cop, then after about twelve years, I moved to a detective role. Six years after that, I was leading a team."

Again, the man paused.

A team? What sort of team? Stitts wondered, but he held his tongue. And, in time, as they made the short drive from the station to the casino, Greg elaborated.

"I was working when the Las Vegas Village shooting took place," he said at last. "I made a calculated decision and moved away from where the shots were being fired. Took a bullet in the leg, and that's that."

But it wasn't all; Stitts could tell by Greg's intonation that there was more to the story, but he also knew that the man was finally done speaking.

Still, Greg had revealed enough for things to start to fall into place. Stitts had been part of the FBI for long enough to know what happened to someone who fled from a gunfight, irrespective of motive.

It meant that you were a coward and that you couldn't be trusted. And, as Stitts was acutely becoming aware, if there was no trust, very little else mattered.

"Let me ask you something, Greg: was Sgt. Theodore present at the shooting?"

Greg shook his head.

"No, he arrived after the fact, headed part of the investigation on the management side. Sgt. Theodore was set to move up to Lieutenant before the incident, but many mistakes were made. And when you have in excess of fifty people dead and no motive after more than a month, fingers start to be pointed internally. A bunch of those fingers ended up aimed at the sergeant."

Another piece to the puzzle, Stitts thought.

Sgt. Theodore was trying to curry political favor by shuttling all resources to the bombings. Putting too much emphasis and bringing the Emerald shootings into the public eye would only open old wounds. Wounds that had clearly stung the man and his career projections.

"What about you?" Greg said suddenly, surprising Stitts.

"Joined the FBI fourteen years ago. Before that, I was in real estate."

He was about to add more but was preoccupied with finding a parking space in The Emerald's underground garage. From the outside, it was as if nothing had happened; the place was packed. Eventually, he gave up and rolled the cruiser into a fire lane.

"I mostly do profiles," he continued, "specialize in—"

Stitts stopped mid-sentence. A man stood smoking by the doorway leading to the elevators. Normally, he wouldn't have paid this any mind, but it had been a while since his last smoke and the sight of it caused him to stare more intently.

There was something about the man, something that was oddly familiar.

"Hey, do you recognize that guy?" he asked.

Greg followed his gaze and rolled down his window.

"I'm not... I'm not sure. My eyes aren't—"

Stitts jammed the car into park and leaped from the vehicle.

"Hey! Hey, buddy, I've got a question—"

Stitts didn't even manage to finish the sentence before the man dropped his cigarette and started to run.

Chapter 26

Given the size of the mansion, and the net worth of the owner, Chase expected a butler to answer the door, Jeeves perhaps, or that creepy bastard Raul who had looked after Clarissa and the late Thomas Smith's place. She was pleasantly surprised when Stu Barnes pulled the large oak door open with his own two hands.

The man was wearing a crisp, white dress shirt, with the sleeves rolled up and the buttons undone to just below his breastbone. His royal-blue pants ended just above the ankle bone, and his sockless feet were buried in black leather driving loafers. The gray hair on his head and cheeks and chin were all neatly brushed.

Chase was nearly startled at how handsome the man was.

"Can I help you?" he asked, with no hint of an accent.

Chase cleared her throat.

"Stu? Stu Barnes?" Chase said, using her poker skills to keep her expression neutral.

The man's eyes narrowed.

"Yeah, I'm Stu Barnes. Who's asking?"

"My name's Chase, Chase Adams. And I'm… well, I heard what happened and I just wanted to come by and say how sorry I was to hear."

For a moment, Chase thought that she'd misread the man, and had incorrectly assumed that he was aware of the murders.

But when the man's blue eyes suddenly went soft, Chase was reassured.

"You must've known Kevin," he said, a hint of lamentation in his voice. Clearly, he was better off backing poker players than becoming one himself. "He was a good man."

Chase found herself nodding, while on the inside she was busy packaging her preconceptions and tossing them into a mental waste bin. She'd expected a businessman with Stu's success to be a ruthless, money-hungry asshole. Instead, the man's first comment wasn't about his missing millions, but about Kevin.

After discarding her incorrect assumptions, Chase's mind switched to the image of Kevin O'Hearn on the board back at the police station. He was in his mid-twenties and had a patchy beard and close-set eyes.

"I met him online, which is where he told me about you. I've never played with him live, but I'm… I dunno, I guess I'm mostly just scared and didn't know where to go."

Stu stepped aside and held the door wide, gesturing for Chase to enter.

"I am scared, too," he admitted.

***

Stu Barnes was clearly hurting, but he hadn't let his guard down completely. In casual conversation, he'd inquired about her online poker name and when he went to fetch coffee, she heard him typing away at his computer. There was only so much you could glean from her poker persona, but with connections, or enough money, of which she suspected Stu had both, you could find out enough.

In the end, however, it mattered little; after speaking with the man for several minutes, she knew that her poker knowledge would come through in only a way that a player's could. There was something about playing mid- to high-level stakes poker that changed you in a way that was difficult to describe.

"I'm just in shock," Stu said, returning with a fresh pot of coffee. "I've known Kevin O'Hearn for... shit, eight years now. We met quarterly to discuss business, but also to shoot the shit. He was planning on proposing to his girlfriend in the fall."

Chase swallowed hard. With poker, it was easy for her to disassociate her emotions; in fact, it was necessary for success. But with people, especially lately, it was becoming more and more difficult.

I'm taking Felix to Sweden. When you get better, you can come visit.

"I only met him online a few years back," she lied; she'd never heard of Kevin before she'd seen his dead body. "He played at the super high-stakes, while I mettle along at the midrange. But once I heard about this..."

"And how *did* you hear about this? I mean, I checked the news and there's nothing about these murders. Either they're working hard to keep things under wrap, or they're focusing on the Planned Parenthood bombing."

It was clear by his tone that he suspected the latter, and was none too happy about it, either.

"The irony is, gamblers and gambling is what makes this town. It's what draws forty million visitors a year, employs tens of thousands of people. Supports the infrastructure, the social programs. And yet, when something like this goes down, the authorities like to push it under the rug, pretend it didn't happen. Silently assert that somehow the gamblers deserved it, that they are degenerates."

Chase couldn't help but be surprised by the man's intuition.

"I have a family friend in the PD—helped him out with some bills a while back," Chase said. "He gives me a little nudge anytime there's something going on in the poker scene. I assure you that they're working on it, but you're right: the focus is on the bombing right now."

"Figures," Stu Barnes said, sipping his coffee. "Normally these private games are safe, especially at The Emerald. A couple of years back several underground poker rings got busted up by the mob in Montréal, but nothing like this. Nothing like flat-out *murder*."

The man stared off into space as he said this, and Chase knew then that he had nothing to do with the attacks.

Something that Stu said also struck a chord with her: *...especially at The Emerald.*

Kevin must have played in one of these private games there before. They had limited video footage from the most recent game, but she wondered if they might have more luck with a previous one. Perhaps the killer or killers staked it out to plan their Houdini act.

Chase made a mental note to ask Stitts to look into this later. She was about to express her disgust at what had happened when Stu suddenly clapped his hands on his thighs and stood.

"You know what? Fuck this coffee. I'm going to have a drink. We'll drink to Kevin."

Stu made his way to the bar near the back of the massive sitting room and promptly returned with two glasses and a bottle of fifty-year-old Balvenie.

"I promised Kevin that we'd pop this bottle when he proposed to his girlfriend," Stu said. His eyes began to water and he turned his back to Chase and tried to wipe the tears away without her noticing. "And now that he's gone... I say we have a drink in his honor."

Chase hadn't prepared for this scenario, and she felt sweat break out on her forehead.

The problem wasn't the alcohol, at least not directly. The common adage was that weed was a gateway drug, but that was complete and utter bullshit. Alcohol was *the* gateway drug by definition. It lowered inhibitions, and when Chase's guard was down, it led to uncomfortable and dangerous situations.

Ones that she'd promised both Dr. Matteo and Stitts that she'd avoid.

Chase was suddenly back at Grassroots bent over the sink, Louisa's pudgy fingers jammed down her throat.

Those types of situations.

And yet, if she said no…

In the end, Stu made the decision for her by pouring two glasses.

"Here," he said, handing her one of them. Chase stared at it for an inordinate amount of time before taking it from the man. Then Stu raised his glass and Chase did the same. "To Kevin."

Chase brought the drink to her lips.

"To Kevin," she repeated quietly.

Chapter 27

STITTS SPRINTED AFTER THE smoking man but, unfamiliar with the surroundings, he quickly found himself lagging behind. He followed through the doors leading to the elevators, but the man made a hard right and entered a stairwell instead.

Stitts opened the door and followed the footsteps upward, taking two at a time.

"Stop!" he shouted. "Stop! FBI!"

The man's only response was sneakers slamming on the individual stairs as he continued upward. Stitts grabbed the railing and hoisted himself up each rung, his breath coming in ragged bursts now.

"Stop!"

Just as Stitts hit the second-floor landing, the door started to close. He managed to keep it open with his foot, and then shoved the pushbar.

The contrast between the empty stairwell and the cornucopia of sounds from The Emerald casino floor was so extreme that it was momentarily disorienting. That, combined with his fatigue, caused Stitts to stumble and he fell onto one knee. And yet, his eyes were still searching for the blond man in the hoodie.

Unlike Stitts, he was still on his feet, not quite running, but moving quickly toward the cashier's desk before taking a hard right around a row of slot machines.

"Wait!" Stitts yelled, but his words were swallowed up by the din of the casino.

Worried that he would lose the man, he pushed himself to his feet and broke into a run again. Only he didn't make it very far: two large men in matching black shirts calmly stepped out of nowhere and blocked his path.

"No running in the casino, sir," the larger of the two men said. His hair was shaved on the sides and a greasy ponytail ran down the back.

Stitts's first instinct was to run around them, but despite their enormous size, they were actually quite agile and quickly blocked his path.

"No running," the man repeated.

Stitts struggled to find his words while trying to catch his breath.

"I'm FBI," he croaked, but either the men didn't understand him, or didn't rightly care.

When he tried to move again, ponytail put a hand on his chest. Stitts slapped it away, but the man grabbed his wrist and twisted it back. Fearing that his arm might snap, Stitts had no choice but to drop back onto one knee.

"I'm FBI," he managed through clenched teeth. "God damn it, I'm FBI! Let me go!"

Instead of replying, ponytail slipped a hand into Stitts's coat and pulled out the wallet containing his badge. He flipped it open and stared at it for a moment before showing it to his partner. They exchanged eyebrow raises before ponytail released his grip on Stitts's wrists.

Stitts immediately jumped to his feet and craned his head around the two beefy security guards, trying to find the smoking man.

He was nowhere in sight.

"Fuck!"

"No running in the casino," ponytail said for a third time. Stitts scowled.

"Are you a fucking robot? Is that all you can say? I was chasing someone, for fuck's sake."

The man simply shrugged, and Stitts looked skyward.

"I need to speak to your manager—I need to speak to Shane McDuff."

Ponytail's eyebrow rose again, only this time it wasn't in surprise, but something akin to fear. Finally, the man seemed to put two and two together: the FBI and what had happened on the seventh floor.

"Well, we didn't know… I mean, we've got strict instructions to not let anyone—"

Stitts shook his head and cut him off.

"I don't give a fuck about that. I need to see Shane McDuff. Are you going to take me to him, or am I going to have to throw your ass in jail for obstruction?"

Chapter 28

SHANE MCDUFF WAS A nervous creature, with eyebrows that were more animated than a cartoon character's. He seemed surprised when Stitts showed up at his office and became visibly agitated when he saw the man's FBI badge. The first twenty or thirty words out of his mouth were related to how he'd already told the police everything that he knew.

Even when Stitts pressed, the man seemed to be locked in the same refrain.

"I need you to tell me what happened last night—I need you to tell me about the shooting."

The man fiddled with a pen in his hand, and Stitts noted that there was blue ink on his fingertips and the webbing between thumb and forefinger.

"I already told the police... I got a call about some noise on the seventh floor—fireworks going off—and I sent my men right up there. They were already gone—whoever did this was gone. And then... and then... and then I called the police."

This wasn't what Stitts intended to ask but decided to let the man continue. It was likely that he was so forthcoming with this information because he had rehearsed it or was reliving it now. Either way, he allowed the man to continue with some gentle probing to see what else he would reveal.

"They were gone?"

Shane shifted uncomfortably.

"Whoever did this... whoever killed them. They were gone. It was horrible... all the blood and..."

They.

Whoever killed them. They *were gone.*

It might've just been a slip of the tongue, but it might've also been a revealing fact.

"What was the time frame between when you got the call about fireworks and when you entered the room?"

Shane shook his head.

"No, I didn't—I didn't enter the room. Not until after. It was one of my security guys. I sent *them* to the room."

"Okay, fine. How much time passed between when you got the call about the fireworks and you sent your security to go check on the room?"

Shane scrunched his nose.

"I... I don't remember. I told this all to the cops, like I said. I was—"

"Approximately how much time, Shane? Ten minutes? An hour?"

Shane shrugged.

"Well, I didn't send my guy right away. I mean, people get prank calls all the time with stuff going on in the rooms. I guess it wasn't until the second call that I sent my security up there. So, I'm guessing... ten or fifteen minutes after the first call?"

In the matter of several minutes, the man's story had already changed. First, Shane had said he sent his men after the phone call, now it was after the *second* call.

"What prompted the second call? Was it more fireworks?"

Shane shook his head.

"No, they said that they heard something like breaking glass or something like that."

Stitts's mind flicked to the broken bottles that surrounded Mike Hartman's fallen body. Chase had suggested that it might be personal against the man, and while he'd initially shrugged this off as improbable, it was looking more likely now. Especially if the killers had gone to his body *after* the shooting was over.

"All right," Stitts began. "Let's take a step back. When did you find out about the game?"

This time, Shane's answer was immediate.

"About two weeks ago, we had a special request from one of the regular guests: Kevin O'Hearn, a high-roller poker player wanting to set up a private game."

"And at these games, do the players use chips or cash?"

Shane suddenly looked constipated.

"*Usually* chips."

Stitts read between the lines. Usually chips because the gaming license required them, but in this case, it had been cash. Chase had already told them as much.

Rather than press Shane on this, Stitts switched course.

"When was the last time, before this one, you held a private game?"

Shane swallowed hard.

"I dunno… not sure. Maybe a year ago? More? I can't remember. You should speak to the other managers, they set them up, too. It's not just me."

Stitts made a mental note of the man's defensiveness and did another about-face.

"What about the people that were working the room? The two men from Luther's investments, the bartender, the dealer, etc."

"We usually have extra security for games with these stakes and contract it out. Luther's is fairly popular. As for the bartender and dealer? These high rollers like to tip big, so I give them to my best guys. Guys who deserve it. Because we like to keep these games on the DL, we usually don't tell the staff until right before the game."

Stitts noted this as well; Shane was the one who made the decisions about the staff, which meant that if Mike was the target, they would only be able to find this out from him.

"Have you used Luther's for security before?"

"Yeah."

"When?"

Shane hesitated, and Stitts could tell that he was almost tripped up. He knew when the last game took place, but for some reason, he wasn't willing to open up about it.

"A while ago; I don't remember."

"Okay, fine. What about video? Do you have video of the hallway? Inside the room?"

Stitts already knew the answer but wanted to gauge Shane's reaction. He'd seen the video of the waiter bringing the food service cart and leaving it at the door. No one came and went until the security guard arrived an hour and a half later to check on the report of fireworks and breaking glass.

"I already gave the hallway footage to the police. But there's no footage inside the room. The poker players wanted it this way."

Shane continued to spin the pen as he spoke and it was starting to annoy Stitts.

"Think you can put the pen down? You're making me nervous."

"S-s-sorry," Shane said, immediately dropping the pen.

Stitts rose to his feet and was about to leave with some parting words when something occurred to him.

"Shane, are there security cameras in this office?"

Shane swallowed.

"*My* office? This one?"

Stitts raised an eyebrow.

"Do you have another office?"

"N-no. This is it. There are no cameras inside."

"What about outside?" Stitts pointed to the door behind him. "Floor cameras that cover the area just outside this office."

"Yeah... I think so, I mean, I'm pretty sure. Why?"

"Just wondering. Think you can do me a favor and send me the tapes of the day before and after the shooting from any cameras that show the office? Would that be alright?"

If Shane looked uncomfortable before, now he looked like a man with underwear full of tics.

"I'll have to ask my boss. He'll have to approve—"

Stitts flashed him a winning smile and then showed the man his badge again.

"You see this? It's a government seal. F-B-I. *That's* your boss. Just send me the tapes, I'm sure he'll understand."

Chapter 29

CHASE GROANED AND OPENED her eyes. She had a thick, fuzzy taste in her mouth as if her tongue had swollen to twice its regular size, and her headache had come in full force.

Confusion washed over her; she had no idea where she was.

Where am I? How did I get here?

Her time back at the crack den in Seattle flashed in her mind then, as did Tyler Tisdale's face. Was she... back *there*? How is that possible?

But she couldn't be. A quick glance at her surroundings didn't reveal refuse and soiled mattresses, drug paraphernalia, but a massive, king-sized bed and stately ceilings.

And yet this did little to calm her panic; her chest was tight and her heart thrummed like a hummingbird stricken with Parkinson's.

Chase sat bolt upright, which only served to tilt the entire world on its axis. She gagged then and bile filled her mouth. It was all she could do to swallow it back down. Along with the acrid bile, she tasted something else on her tongue: scotch. *Expensive* scotch. Fifty-year-old scotch.

The pieces finally fell into place.

With another hard swallow, she turned her head to her right and saw Stu Barnes. He was lying beside her on the bed, eyes closed. He was wearing silk pajama bottoms, but no shirt.

My God, Chase, he's old enough to be your dad.

Glancing down at herself, she was surprised to see that she was fully dressed. After waiting another minute for the nausea to pass, she slipped silently off the bed and made her way toward the door. Before leaving, however, Chase peered back into the room and stared at Stu for a moment.

I came here... I came here to find out about Kevin, to see if Stu might've been involved in the heist and murders. And I leave here... like this?

Tears threatened to overwhelm her then, and her ex-husband's voice echoed in her head.

Get well, Chase. That's all we want for you. Get well, and then you can see Felix again.

As she made her way downstairs, Chase felt shame envelop her like a frigid embrace. When she saw that it was now dark outside, her shame became a cradle of disgust.

Stitts was right not to trust me. And I was right not to trust myself.

Only when she was safely inside her partner's rental did she dare take a full breath and pull out her phone.

There were no calls or texts from her husband, of course, or a voicemail from her son. But she hadn't expected any. They had moved on, and she was struggling to do the same. But what hurt her most in that moment was the fact that Stitts hadn't called. She'd missed their dinner plans, and he hadn't even reached out to her.

The one person in this world who still cared for her finally seemed to have moved on as well.

Chapter 30

STITTS HAD COMPLETELY FORGOTTEN about Greg Ivory and nearly stumbled into the man as he turned the corner leading to the stairwell.

"Shit, sorry," Stitts grumbled.

Greg just shook his head and raised a palm as if to say, *no problem*.

"Did you catch the kid?"

Stitts hesitated for a moment. After his 'interesting' conversation with Shane McDuff, he'd forgotten all about the blond man smoking a cigarette.

"No, fuck. He got away. I thought… I thought he looked like someone from the board. Mike, maybe, but I'm not sure."

"I didn't get a good look. These eyes ain't what they used to be. My contact reached out, said he compiled some information about Mike Hartman and his family."

Stitts stopped mid-step.

"Family?"

Greg indicated the elevator and Stitts changed course.

"Yeah. Apparently, his father used to work for the casino. Died a couple of months back from a heart attack."

The elevator pinged and they stepped inside.

"Interesting. Do me a favor? See if he can dig up anything on Shane McDuff, the manager, as well."

"Anything, in particular, you're looking for?"

"Yeah, when the last 'secret' poker game was held."

"I'll see what he can do. And the manager? How is he?"

"Oh, you know, he's a piece of shit," Stitts said as the elevator doors opened and they made their way toward Greg's squad car. "Slimy bastard, lying about some—no, not some, *most* things. I'm guessing he's always like that, though."

As they approached the car, Stitts noticed something on the windshield. Only when they got closer did he realize that it was a parking ticket.

"Seriously?" he said as he picked it up. It was a $350 fine for parking in the fire lane.

Stitts looked at Greg, but the man seemed unsurprised.

"I guess they know my tag number," he offered as an explanation.

Stitts made sure to put the ticket into his pocket and then got into the driver's seat. With a sigh, he glanced at his cell phone.

It was coming up on 6:30 and there was still no word from Chase. The way he saw it, she had to call him. After all, she was the one who had taken his car. She was the one with… *issues*. And yet, despite telling himself this, he had to fight the urge to reach out to her.

There was no word from the hospital, either.

"Where to now?" Greg asked.

Stitts mulled this over for a moment. He didn't want to go back to the cramped office with Greg, nor did he feel like running into the ATF or DoD assholes.

"You know what? I'm going to check out the crime scene one more time," he said at last. "You're welcome to join or feel free to go back to the station. I can get a ride later."

Greg stretched his leg.

"I think I'm better off just sitting here. Twig is flaring up something fierce. I can start to go through the stuff my contact sent me about Mike Hartman. See if there's anything of interest."

Stitts opened the door again. He was about to exit when he turned back to the passenger seat.

"Thanks, Greg."

The man nodded.

He was turning out to be a valuable asset and something told Stitts that the blowback Greg was getting from the rest of the LVMPD was unwarranted. And yet, there was a part of the story, an important part, that the man was unwilling to share.

Yet.

***

Stitts took the elevator to the seventh floor and when the doors opened he was immediately stopped by a uniformed officer. He flashed his badge and the man let him through. A network of yellow police tape crisscrossed the hallway and Stitts had to bob and weave to move through it. As he walked, Stitts looked around, observing first the ceiling, then the stairway door at the far end of the corridor. Eventually, his eyes found the camera nestled just above the door trim.

So distracted was he, that Stitts nearly bowled over a CSI tech who was crouched and working on the food service tray.

"Sorry," he grumbled. The tech didn't even look up. As he moved toward the door that was wedged open, Stitts noticed that the silver platter on which the food lay was completely full; there didn't appear to be a fry missing, let alone a bite from the burger. This struck him as odd as the food was delivered long before the first shot.

Pausing outside the room, he fired off a quick text to Greg.

See if you can find out who ordered the food to the room prior to the shooting.

Donning plastic shoe covers by the door, Stitts finally entered the crime scene. The bodies had since been removed, but CSI was still going over every item in the place using potions and lotions and powders and whatever other alchemy they had at their disposal to uncover evidence. As Greg had informed them earlier, so far, they'd come up with zilch.

Ignoring the techs in the room, Stitts walked the perimeter, trying to absorb the scene. He attempted to do what Chase did, to breathe everything in and then spontaneously regurgitate it as a vision later. But as time passed, he found himself more focused on Chase than the scene.

It was too soon for her to be back in the field, he knew this, just as Director Hampton had known it back in Quantico.

But he'd already lost one partner and Chase was... *special*, in ways he was only beginning to understand.

Stitts eventually found himself by the windows absently rapping on them with his knuckles, staring down at the bright lights of Las Vegas below.

If he had to get in and out of the room without using the doors the only other options were the windows. The only problem was, they were completely unblemished, solid and impossible to open.

"Beautiful, isn't it?" someone said from his right.

Stitts jumped and he shot the tech a look that was equal parts shock and disgust.

It wasn't beautiful; they were standing in a room where less than twenty-four hours ago a massacre occurred.

It wasn't beautiful, it was horrific.

"Just splendid," he replied pushing his lips together tightly.

"Yeah, nice of the window cleaners to come by and give them a good scrub."

Stitts nodded and subtly suggested with his body language that he wanted to be left alone. The tech nodded and started back toward the bar when Stitts thought of something.

He reached over and grabbed the tech by the shoulder, this time startling him.

"You were here before?" he asked sharply.

The man gave him a queer look.

"Before what?"

Stitts fought his frustration.

"When did the window cleaners come?"

The man shrugged.

"An hour ago? I really don't know; me 'n' Archie over there took a late lunch—well, I mean, it was *our* lunch but not 'lunchtime'. You know how it is in Vegas, Anyways, when we got back, they were leaving. Saw the carriage going down."

Stitts turned his attention downward, not at the city street this time, but at the building itself. He thought he could make out the dark outline of a window carriage as it nestled on the ground below. Dusk had settled over Las Vegas, and the casinos cast long shadows.

"An hour ago…" Stitts muttered. "An hour ago…"

Something felt wrong about that, but it wasn't until he pulled away from the window that it clicked. The cleaners were on the list of people they had to interview because they'd done the windows the day *before* the murders.

And now they were back again, the day after.

"Shit," Stitts swore, hurrying from the room. He had to catch the window cleaners before they took off like the man with the cigarette in the parking garage.

"You okay?" the tech hollered after him. "Is it—*holy shit!*"

Stitts was almost out the door when the man's inflection drew him back.

"What? What is it?"

The tech extended a finger to an area just off the strip.

"I think… I think a bomb just went off."

Chapter 31

GRIDLOCK. ABSOLUTE, UTTER GRIDLOCK.

At first, Chase thought that this was the norm for the Las Vegas strip on a busy Friday night. But when the sky erupted in a mixture of red and white and blue lights, Chase knew differently.

Something had happened.

It took Chase a few moments to realize that the traffic on the strip was being caused, at least in part, by the fact that all the side streets seemed to be blocked by police cruisers. It took her fifteen minutes to finally make it to the next side street and when she did, she took it. Before she'd even made it to the police car, an officer approached, his hands held out in front of him as if he were trying to push her back using only air pressure.

"You can't come down here; street's closed."

Chase quickly flashed her badge.

"What's going on?"

"Looks like there was another bombing," the officer said, leaning in close to her open window. "This time at a church."

A Church? First the Planned Parenthood building and now a church? Wasn't it usually those who frequented churches that bombed Planned Parenthood? Someone's ideology is mighty messed up.

"For real? A church?"

"Yeah, the church is known around here as the Queer Jesus church. Apparently, it's one of the few that supports gay rights and gay marriages."

And that explains that, Chase thought.

"You want to go through?"

Chase looked at the officer for a moment and then turned her attention to the commotion in the distance.

She didn't *want* to go in. The truth was, Chase didn't give a shit about this, especially if it, like the bombing at Planned Parenthood, resulted in zero injuries or deaths. But going back the other way, fighting traffic for another hour was even less desirable.

"Yeah, I'll take a look," she said at last. The officer stepped aside, making his way to his car and reversing so that Chase's vehicle could squeeze by.

She was stopped twice more on her way to the church, both times she showed her badge and got through without any difficulty.

Eventually, when she could continue no further by car, Chase parked and got out, pressing her hands deep into her pockets. To her right, behind a large bomb squad van, was the church, the front door of which had been reduced to a char. The damage seemed limited to the front stoop, however, as the interior looked barely touched. And, judging by the three empty ambulances to her left, Chase was fairly certain that this, like the previous bombing, hadn't intended to injure.

"First Planned Parenthood, now the Church of Gay Jesus," she muttered under her breath. "What the hell is the point of this?"

Chase was in the process of turning back to her car when she froze.

Jeremy Stitts was standing not fifteen feet from her, his eyes locked on hers. He wasn't smiling.

Stitts had every right to be angry with her, given that, once again, she'd taken his car and left him for hours. Not to mention the fact that it was nearly nine now, and they had planned to eat dinner together at 6:30. And yet, all she felt in that moment was anger.

How dare he judge me? He's just a condescending prick like the rest of them. Like Agent Martinez, like Director Hampton, like those assholes in Alaska and Chicago and Boston. It's only a matter of time before he starts calling me ma'am.

Gritting her teeth, Chase turned away from her partner and hurried back to her car. She was just pulling the door open when Stitts's voice reached her.

"Chase! Chase, wait!"

Chase took a deep breath and stood with one foot in and one foot out of the vehicle as Stitts approached.

"Where were you?" he demanded.

Dusk had transitioned into night and in Las Vegas the millions of tiny suns that made up the strip, cast Stitts in an eerie, twinkling glow.

"I told you," Chase snapped. "I went to see Stu Barnes, to see if he knew anything about the game, if he was involved."

Stitts's face twisted.

"That was more than five hours ago."

"No shit," she spat back.

Stitts recoiled as if he'd been struck and, for a brief moment, Chase regretted her words. He wasn't like Martinez, he wasn't like any of them.

He was different.

"Did you... do you need help?" Stitts asked under his breath.

Any regrets Chase felt in that moment dissolved.

"That's none of your fucking business, Stitts. I don't need you to look after me, look out for me, protect me, or any of that bullshit."

But that was a lie, too. It *was* his business because she was certain that his ass was on the line this time as well. And she did need somebody to look out for her. But this understanding did nothing to stem her anger.

"I'm sorry, it's just... I was worried."

"Worried about what? About your job? About whatever alt-right asshole blew up this church? Or are you worried about finding the bastards who murdered eleven people last night? Is that what you're worried about? Because if not, if you're worried about me, don't waste your damn time. It's not worth it."

Stitts said nothing.

"Stop doing that," she snarled. "I'm not one of your fucking suspects."

Stitts just stared, and Chase was helpless to stop herself from venting.

"You worried that I won't be able to help you by touching the dead? Well, let me tell you something, Stitts. You really want to know what I felt when I touched the bartender's arm? When I grabbed Mike Hartman's tattoo? Hmmm?"

She waited for him to react, but Stitts just remained stone-faced. Sweat was not just forming on her brow now but was leaving wet streaks down her face.

"*Nothing*. That's what I saw, Stitts; absolutely fucking nothing. I touched his arm and nothing happened. I have no clue what went on in that room, and if I can't... if I can't..." her voice hitched and it took considerable effort to finish that sentence. "...and if I can't do that, Stitts, I can't do anything."

The tears started to flow then, tears not just because whatever strange ability she once had was gone, but tears because of what she'd done with Stu Barnes, the drinks she'd had at his place, missing another rendezvous with Stitts.

Her tears were her shame, her anger at herself most of all, manifested.

"I know," he said softly. "I know."

Despite the way she'd treated him when Chase collapsed into his chest and sobbed, Stitts wrapped his arms around her and held her tight.

Chapter 32

"Is she going to be all right?" Greg Ivory asked, leaning into the window of Stitts's car. They had separated at the bombing, with Greg taking his squad car back to the station, while Stitts and Chase had taken his.

Shortly after they'd left, Chase had dozed off in the passenger seat. She looked exhausted and Stitts smelled alcohol on her breath at the scene, but there was something more alarming about her than that.

It was the way she'd reacted to him, the visceral, misplaced aggression that was most telling. Even though before her breakdown Chase had been shouting at him, he wasn't the target; *she* was.

Stitts cleared his throat.

"She'll be okay," he said, even though he was far from certain. No matter how hard he tried to help her, there was no guarantee that she would ever be okay.

Chase roused at the sound of his voice.

"Georgina? Is that you?" she asked sleepily.

Stitts swallowed the lump in his throat and silently indicated to Greg that he would meet him inside the station.

"No, Chase, it's me, Stitts."

Chase blinked once, twice, and then sat up straight.

With a sigh, she looked around, her eyes eventually falling on the LVMPD station.

"Well, what are we waiting for, then? Let's get in there and figure out who our Houdini is."

***

"So, care to give me an update, or what?" Chase said.

Stitts stared at her for a moment, wanting to ask her the same thing, to inquire about her meeting with Stu. Fighting this urge, he turned to Greg instead.

"Greg? Did you find out about the food?"

Greg looked at them both with a curious expression on his face and shifted his weight onto the cane before answering.

"Mike Hartman ordered the food to the room."

Chase made a face.

"The bartender ordered food? Really? That doesn't make sense; what bartender orders food for himself at a high-stakes poker game?"

"Maybe he ordered it for one of the other players," Stitts offered.

Greg quickly quashed that idea.

"I've got it on pretty good authority that it was for him. In fact, it was the same meal he ordered pretty much every night when he was on break: hamburger and fries, no onion, no pickle."

"But he didn't eat it."

All eyes were on Stitts now.

"I went back to the scene—the meal was untouched."

"That's strange," Chase said, summing up their collective thoughts. "Anything else?"

"Neither the waiter who delivered the food to the room, a Tony Ballucci, nor the window washer, Peter Doherty, clocked in to work today."

At the mention of the window washer, Stitts's eyes flicked to the board.

"Fuck," he said under his breath. "That's him."

Chase turned to face him.

"That's who? *Who's* who?"

Stitts walked over and tapped Peter's face.

"This is the guy that ran from me at the casino. His hair is blond now, but I'm sure of it."

"Ran from you?"

Stitts shrugged.

"Long story. Never caught him."

"You can blame your new habit for that," Chase said.

Stitts frowned.

"Peter may not have clocked into work, but he was definitely there. *And* there's something else. Someone washed the windows on the seventh floor today."

Chase looked incredulous.

"Really? How often do they clean the windows at The Emerald? The hotel must have… what? A thousand of them? Is the manager OCD or something?"

Stitts pictured Shane's hand, covered in splotches of ink.

"Definitely not."

"So why would the cleaners clean the same windows two days apart?"

"Maybe they were snapping pictures? Videos for TMZ, maybe?" Greg suggested.

Stitts rocked his head side to side and said as he contemplated this.

"Maybe. But you'd think that it was highly regulated. I mean, they have to set up the carriage on the roof, etc."

Chase threw her arms up.

"Oh, great. So now we've got a starving bartender who doesn't eat his meal and an overzealous window cleaner who may or may not have been at work today. Fucking Sherlock Holmes, we ain't."

Chase's words hung in the air of the small, cramped office for several minutes before she broke it again.

"And we're no closer to solving the most important question."

"Which is?" Greg asked.

"How the *fuck* our killer got into, and out of, the room. If we can figure that out, I'm pretty sure we'd be able to narrow down our pool of suspects."

"Well," Stitts replied. "Unless someone managed the unlikely task of somehow altering the video, nobody entered or left that room within an hour and a half of the murders. And unless the guns were somehow dissolved, it can't be a warped murder/suicide, either. The only thing that entered the room was the—*shit*."

He hurried over to his laptop on Greg's desk.

"What is it?" Chase asked. "What?

Instead of answering, Stitts brought up a grainy video of the seventh-floor hallway. He skipped forward until Tony Ballucci appeared on screen, pushing the food service cart.

"The cart…" Stitts said at last. "The cart is the *only* thing that entered and exited the room."

Chapter 33

"SEE THAT?" CHASE ASKED, leaning close to the computer monitor. "See how he has to shift his hips to get the cart moving? If it really is just a hollow cart covered in the tablecloth, with a burger and fries on top, why is he straining to get it out of the elevator?"

Chase looked to Stitts, who nodded.

"Yeah, I see it. Now watch as he goes down the hall, knocks on the door and then one of Luther's men brings it in."

On screen, the video played out exactly how Stitts described it. He fast-forwarded until the hotel security—a cube of a man with a long ponytail that ran down his back—exited the elevator and made his sweet ass time toward the room in question.

"You thinking what I'm thinking?" Stitts asked.

"I'm sure as hell not; I don't have a fucking clue what you guys are talking about," Greg said.

Chase ignored him and focused her attention on the monitor.

"You think this is some sort of Trojan horse type thing? The killer was brought in on this trolley, shot up the room and killed everybody, and then escaped somehow?"

Stitts shrugged.

"It would explain why Luther's men were caught off guard."

"Keep going, keep it running."

The security guard knocked on the door and then waited. A minute or so later, he used his card to open the door and stepped inside. Almost immediately, he reappeared, stumbling down the hall toward the elevator, walkie pressed to his lips. After he was gone, Stitts fast-forwarded until the police arrived, then kept the video going in double-speed until CSI appeared on the scene.

"There's no way our killer hid under the cart in the room the whole time. Not with all these cops and CSI coming back and forth. There's no way; that's ridiculous," Chase said.

"Not unless maybe one of the techs or officers were in on it," Stitts replied with a grin.

He slowed the video to real-time when a CSI tech rolled the cart out of the room and pushed it against the wall just outside the door. Even though Chase thought that Stitts was grasping at straws, she waited with bated breath as the video continued.

"There," Stitts exclaimed, pausing the video.

The same tech who had pushed the trolley out of the room appeared to look around before reaching down and lifting the tablecloth. Despite how unlikely Stitts's theory was, Chase *wanted* to see a man under there, perhaps one dressed in army fatigues, an AR-15 in his lap. That would, at least, be something to go on, solve at least part of the mystery. But the area beneath the cart was empty.

"Shit," Stitts muttered under his breath. "Where the fuck did they go? How did they get out of the room?"

Chase noticed that he was still using *they* based on the greaseball manager's slip of the tongue. She, on the other hand, wasn't so certain that it was more than one person.

"The windows. It has to be the windows," Greg said. "Unless they pulled an *Inside Job* and built a false wall."

Stitts sighed.

"The room matches the schematic. Besides, the cops have been over every square inch of the place. As for the windows, I checked them myself. They don't open, and they are in perfect condition—they're solid."

Chase walked back to her chair and slumped in it, rubbing her temples.

"Everyone involved in this thing seems so damn shady, but nobody has a motive," she said.

"They all had the universal motive, Chase: cash," Stitts said.

Chase shrugged.

"I guess," she said, picturing Mike Hartman's bloody face in her mind. "Just seems like overkill. We've got eleven dead people, anywhere between twelve and fifteen million dollars missing, and a killer who vanished into thin air."

"Killers," Stitts said. Chase raised an eyebrow and Stitts continued, "when I spoke to the manager, he said *they*. As in *they* got away."

They sat in silence for several seconds before Stitts got to his feet.

"I need a smoke," he said, before turning to Greg. "Wait, back in the elevators at The Emerald, you said something about your contact compiling information about Mike Hartman's family?"

Greg nodded.

"Yeah, not sure if it means anything, but Mike Hartman's father, Harry Hartman, used to be a dealer at The Emerald."

"Seriously? Harry Hartman?" Chase said. "Yeesh."

Her comment went ignored.

"And? Does he still work there?"

Greg turned his attention to his phone for a moment before answering.

"Nope. Died about two months ago. Heart attack. Actually happened on casino property."

Chase's interest was piqued.

"Anything else?"

"Nope… wait, only that his father used to deal at some of these private poker games."

Stitts's eyes narrowed.

"Let me guess, he was one of Shane McDuff's favorites."

Greg shrugged.

"No record of that here. And no record of when the last private game was held, either."

"What do you mean, no record? Shane admitted to holding other games, he was just lying about not remembering when the last one took place."

"I'll have my contact keep digging."

Chase's phone buzzed in her pocket, and she pulled it out. There was a single text message from *ATM* again.

Another game—tomorrow 10 a.m., two-million-dollar buy-in. The Emerald.

Chase felt a knot in her stomach.

Already? How the hell can they be so brazen?

"Good. Also, I asked the manager for footage outside his office before and after the murders, but he was reluctant. See if you can get your guy to come up with that." Stitts tapped his chin. "One more thing, I'm not ready to give up on this food service cart thing just yet. See if you can get video footage of where it came from, its path from the kitchen to the room."

Greg agreed.

"Chase, you think we should bring in the manager? The window washer, if we can find him?"

Another game… the killers wouldn't dare hitting another game so soon, would they? But if Stitts is right and the only motive is money…

"Chase?"

One thing was for certain; if they did strike again, Chase wanted to be there.

"Chase? Earth to Chase."

Chase snapped out of her head and looked up, staring across the room at Stitts.

"Yeah? What is it?"

"I asked if you think that we should bring in the window washer and the manager and grill them a little."

Chase shook her head.

"No, not quite yet. Let's just keep an eye on them for now until we have more to go on."

And if they're involved, I don't want to tip them off that we know about this new game.

Chapter 34

"**You can't be serious,** Chase," Stitts said. "I mean, you didn't even tell me what the hell Stu Barnes said the first time you went to go meet him."

The last thing Chase wanted to do was lie to her partner *again*, but she didn't see any other way out of this. If she told him what she was really planning on doing, Stitts would almost certainly intervene. And based on how far she'd already pushed him, she wasn't sure to what lengths he might go to stop her.

For a moment, Chase was back in her shitty apartment in Quantico, holding her psych and medical evaluations, both of which she'd failed, and Stitts was standing before her.

You have two choices, Chase… go to prison or go to rehab.

At the time, she'd been certain that he wouldn't let her go to prison, but now, she wasn't so sure.

It's for his own good, she told herself.

Another lie, of course.

It was for *her* own good.

"Stu just texted me and said there's been some chatter about a new player who wants a high-stake game, having just come into some money."

It was a shitty lie, but she hoped that Stitts knew so little about how the poker scene worked, especially when it came to private games and backers, that he might go for it.

The man's face underwent a series of changes then, shifting from what was clearly anger, to something else. Something she couldn't quite place.

"And this guy… this investor, Stu Barnes? He wants to meet you tonight?"

Chase shook her head.

"No, not tonight. Tomorrow, sometime. Morning. But right now… right now, Stitts, I need some sleep. I'm fucking tired."

And hungover. And ashamed. And guilty.

"Should I get my own room?" she asked.

Stitts sighed and, at that moment, Chase knew that she had him.

"I've already arranged rooms for us at a hotel off the strip," he said dejectedly.

Rooms; plural. That was good. That was *better*.

"All right, send me the address," Chase said as she made her way to the door.

Stitts rubbed his eyes and then eventually nodded. For what felt like the thousandth time, Chase wondered why he was doing this, why the man was willing to risk everything for her, someone who, in reality, he barely knew.

Guilt caused her solar plexus to clench, but she forced the ball down into the pit of her stomach with the rest of her emotions.

"I'll take you there," Stitts offered.

When Chase started to shake her head, Stitts snapped at her.

"For fuck's sake, Chase! Let me do that at least. I'll take you to the hotel, check us in, then I'll be out of your fucking hair, if that's what you want."

Chase eyed him suspiciously and then looked over her shoulder at Greg, who was pretending not to listen, but clearly was.

Stitts lowered his gaze.

"Please," he said quietly. "There's something I need to tell you."

Chase couldn't tell if this was just a ploy to keep an eye on her, but she couldn't see how she could wriggle her way out of this one. She was about to agree when someone appeared at the door, red-faced and out of breath.

The man didn't even bother knocking, and it took a moment for Chase to realize who it was. It seemed like they'd met months ago, even though it had been less than a day when he'd offered his office to them.

"Hey, FBI guys, I need your help," Sgt. Theodore said. "We need a profile on this bomber."

Stitts and Chase exchanged looks before the latter shrugged.

"That's your domain, Stitts. Looks like I'll be going to the hotel by myself after all."

***

The hotel was also a lie, she had no intention of heading there, at least not quite yet. Despite everything that had happened, there was one thing that nagged her most of all, something that she just couldn't seem to get out of her head.

She needed to know; she needed to know if she could *see*. And the only place she could do that was at the morgue.

A simple Google search revealed where it was, and her FBI badge got her in the door. Claiming to need to see Mike Hartman's body again for the case, the tech, who seemed equally enamored by Chase as he was her badge, didn't hesitate in taking her to the room.

The smell of antiseptic in the room was strong and it caused her tired eyes to start watering immediately upon entering. The room itself was much larger than the one she'd visited in Alaska, but the sensation Chase experienced was the same: a heaviness to the air, a stillness that could only be had in death.

"Mike Hartman's body is near the back," the man said, pointing toward a row of lockers that flanked the rear wall. "Everything is arranged by name, but I should warn you that the victim's mother? Well, she's a real fucking treat, let me tell you—pardon my French."

Chase thanked the man and, when he was gone, she moved toward the lockers he'd indicated. As she did, her thoughts turned to the woman, Ms. Hartman, with her rheumy eyes and raw nose. The way she'd been so adamant about her son's watch had been strange, but everything about this case was strange.

Chase's eyes homed in on the label with Mike Hartman's name written on it in bold letters.

Her hand hesitated before opening the locker, however.

What happens if I open this box, touch his skin, and nothing happens? Even now, hungover as shit, what am I going to do if nothing happens?

Chase took a deep, shuddering breath.

That wasn't the only problem, of course. Perhaps even more frightening was the prospect of what she would do if something *did* happen.

Don't be such a pussy, she scolded herself. *Open the door.*

Imbued with a false sense of courage and a lack of good sense, Chase did just that.

Chapter 35

STITTS WAS SO ANGRY that he could barely see straight. He thought that if he rescued Chase the way he had and got her back on board, that she would be more amenable to his rules. To *their* rules, to the rules that applied to the FBI and every other citizen living in the United States of America.

If anything, she was more obstinate now than she had been before.

And Stitts was pretty sure she was using, too. Maybe not the hard stuff, not yet, but he'd seen this before with someone else that he loved dearly. If she continued down this path, it was only a matter of time before she slipped back into her heroin addiction. And how long after that would he be called to her house only to find her with lipstick on her cheek giving away her things to some punks on the street?

For his mother, it had taken more than a decade. With Chase, he feared that he'd be identifying her corpse long before that happened.

And now *this*. This *bullshit*; being dragged into another case that he wanted nothing to do with.

"I can give you a preliminary profile if you let me have the case files for a few hours," he snarled. "But that's all I can do. You've only given me one guy, my partner is exhausted, and I have eleven dead bodies with no suspects. And what've you got? A couple of cherry bombs going off in sensitive locations with no injuries."

Sgt. Theodore said nothing; he just led them to a conference room on the second floor.

"The files, Sergeant, I need the—"

Stitts stopped when he saw that the conference room was packed with people. He picked out Duane and Josh, as well as other ATF and DoD agents. The rest of the room was full of uniformed officers.

"I—I need some time," he said, his anger fading. "I need time to put together a profile. You need to give me the files so that I can sketch it out."

Sgt. Theodore shook his head.

"We don't have time. This is escalating and before we know it, we're going to have some dead bodies on our hands."

"Dead bodies? *Dead bodies?* We already have dead bodies... eleven of them. All you've got is a few broken windows."

Sgt. Theodore grabbed his arm and spun him around.

"I invited you guys, the FBI, to Las Vegas to help. And that's what I need now: help," the man hissed.

Stitts narrowed his eyes and glared at the sergeant's hand that gripped his upper forearm.

"Let go of my arm," he said in a calm, flat voice.

Seeing the look in his eyes, the sergeant released his grip and took a step back.

"I'm sorry," Sgt. Theodore grumbled. "Just under so much pressure to close this goddamn thing."

And to get your promotion to lieutenant, the one that you were on track for before you fucked up during the Village shooting, Stitts thought, recalling what Greg had told him back at The Emerald. *That's what this is really about.*

Stitts wanted to tell the man to fuck off, but he knew that it wouldn't be long before this got back to Quantico and Director Hampton. And given the trajectory of their own investigation, and Chase's problems, he had the sneaking suspicion that they might need the director on their side in the future.

In the *near* future.

Stitts swallowed his pride and took a deep breath.

"You got two bombs, one outside Planned Parenthood the other at a church that supported gay rights?"

The sergeant nodded.

"Yeah, the church is known as the Queer Jesus Church or something like that."

Stitts looked at the room full of expectant agents and started to think that maybe this distraction would be a good thing. Perhaps an easy profile such as this one was just what he needed to take his mind off things, give him a new perspective on his own case. Worst-case scenario, he would establish some credibility with Theodore and his men in the rare event that *they* needed *them* in the future.

But if he grabs me like that again…

"All right, lead me inside."

Sgt. Theodore made his way toward the door and pulled it wide, and all eyes were suddenly on FBI Agent Jeremy Stitts.

"This is the FBI profiler I was telling you about," the sergeant said in a booming voice. "And he's here to help us. Agent Stitts?"

Chapter 36

MIKE HARTMAN WAS PALER than Chase remembered him, which was the result of having been laid out on a refrigerated slab for the last twenty-four hours or so. And yet, in some ways, he was the exact same, despite the fact that he had been stripped naked. Rather than touch the man right away, Chase observed his wounds—the bullet holes in his chest, his face which had been reduced to a bloody mess, his hands and fingers that had been chewed ragged by glass, the tattoo on his right forearm of the sparrow that his mother had used to identify him.

Chase swallowed hard and closed her eyes. She tried to picture the scene in which she found the man, lying behind the bar, his hand still wrapped around a shattered tequila bottle.

Do it, Chase. Touch him.

Chase's eyes snapped open and she reached out and grabbed the man's wrist just above the tattoo.

Then she inhaled sharply.

She could feel the texture of Mike's skin, which was drier than a living person's, and also the prickle of recently shaved hairs.

But that was all she felt, all she saw. Chase closed her eyes again and redoubled her concentration. She envisioned the food service cart being rolled into the room, a man leaping out, spraying the room with automatic gunfire. Bullets lodging into furniture, the walls, shattering the windows.

Chase tried so hard that she eventually saw stars.

And yet these weren't visions; they were only the stirrings of her imagination, which quickly evaporated like drops of water in a scalding cast-iron pan.

She opened her eyes and gripped Mike's wrist so hard that her fingers started to ache.

"Come on, show me what you see," she pleaded through gritted teeth.

Still nothing happened. Chase wasn't transported elsewhere, she didn't get that sense of vertigo and nausea that came with her visions—she felt nothing. Nothing, aside from cold, dead flesh.

"Fuck!"

Chase let go of the man's arm and it smacked loudly on the metal tray, a sound that echoed in the otherwise silent room.

Still nothing.

With a sharp intake of breath, she touched his abdomen with two fingers right near one of the bullet holes.

When that didn't inspire any visions, Chase went back to his wrist again.

Sweating now, Chase rolled the body into the locker, only she shoved it too hard and it banged back open again. One of Mike's legs slipped off the gurney, and she was forced to flip it back on. After closing the locker more gently this time, she looked around the room.

The locker beside Mike's belonged to Kevin O'Hearn, and her thoughts turned to Stu Barnes and the drinks they had shared.

What the fuck am I doing? Chase wondered.

Without thinking, she started to pull Kevin's locker open, intent on trying her trade with another dead body, when a shout from behind her drew her attention.

Chase whipped around and saw the man who had let her into the morgue standing with his back to the glass door. He was holding his hands up, yelling at someone, telling them that they couldn't go in there, that they weren't authorized.

Through gaps in the man's gestures, she caught sight of the assailant.

It was Ms. Hartman.

"My son is in there! He's *rotting* in there! I need to claim his body!"

"I'm sorry, but his body hasn't been released by the police yet. You'll have to wait until the—"

"Out of my way!" Ms. Hartman shouted. When she reached for the clerk's arm, Chase hurried to the door and pulled it wide. The man all but stumbled inside, which ended up working in Chase's favor. She easily slipped in front of him and confronted the grieving woman.

"Ms. Hartman," Chase said. "My name's Chase Adams, and I'm with—"

The woman scowled at her. She looked much worse than earlier that morning when she'd stormed into the police station. Then, her hair had been pulled into a tight ponytail and she looked decently put together. Now, however, Ms. Hartman wasn't wearing any makeup, revealing mottled cheeks, and her hair was frizzy and unkempt.

"I know who you are. You're supposed to find the person who murdered my son and find his watch—I want his watch back. His dad gave him that watch, and that's all he cared about in the world."

Chase sighed. She'd forgotten all about the watch, which was just another strange element to this case that just didn't seem to fit.

"We're trying our—"

"Yeah, your 'best.' That's what everyone tells me: *'We're doing our best to find your son's killer.'* I've heard all this crap before. *'Oh, we'll do an investigation into your husband's death.'*

You know what comes out of you people doing your 'best?' Nothing; absolutely, fucking *nothing*."

Chase offered a cautious glance over her shoulder to the cowering man behind her who was clearly terrified of Ms. Hartman.

Then she was taken back to an earlier time, a time when she had visited Clarissa Smith. She recalled how irate the woman had been, how confused that her husband had been murdered.

Despite the obvious differences between the two, Chase sympathized with this woman as she had once Ms. Smith.

"How about you and I go for a drink, Ms. Hartman? Just sit down, have a drink, and talk. What do you think about that?"

The woman was taken aback by this and simply opened her mouth but didn't say anything.

Chase stepped forward and put a gentle hand on her shoulder.

"Come on, let's go have a drink."

Chapter 37

"WE ARE MOST LIKELY looking for a white male between the ages of twenty-five and forty, who was brought up in an abusive environment or is gay. Perhaps both," Stitts began. "The fact that the bombing locations were targeted on off-peak hours, coupled with the fact that no one was hurt, suggests that this person is testing the waters. These are likely some of the very first crimes that he has committed, which were, in part—"

"Will they progress?" Sgt. Theodore asked. "Become more dangerous? Will he target more highly populated areas?"

Stitts frowned.

"Please hold your questions until I'm done," he said. "It is also likely that our unsub's father or uncle or grandfather—or whoever the patriarchal figure in the unsub's life was–either died recently or was incarcerated. Either way, this loss was a trigger for these recent acts. Given the specific targets, it is safe to assume that the unsub is seeking blame for what happened to his father. While statistics indicate that the unsub is working alone, it is highly likely that he's receiving coaching from somebody or is taking part in online groups that foster hatred for a wide range of liberal values, including, but not limited to, abortion, Black Lives Matter, and Islamaphobia. The unsub was probably part of the middle class, but his father's situation likely affected his financial security. Moreover, the unsub has strong convictions, and yet—"

Stitts paused for a second, his mind whirring.

Even though he was providing a generic profile, one that he'd hastily put together on the fly, something about what he'd just said struck him as important.

The man has strong convictions...

Did he, though? He didn't kill anyone, at least not yet. On the other hand, the man he was chasing had killed eleven people, stolen millions, and then vanished. Now *that* was a man with convictions.

Stitts mulled this over for a moment, not caring that the men that packed the room were staring at him, waiting for him to continue.

He found himself asking the same questions that Chase had posed a day ago. Only now he was considering them with more conviction.

Why *had* their unsub killed the poker players? They would have posed no threat, especially after taking out the men from Luther's Investments. Chase already implied that even though the sums were as gaudy as they were, it wasn't even the poker players' money.

So why kill them all?

For some reason, Stitts hadn't bothered putting together a profile of the hotel room killer, mostly because there had been so many confusing facts and missing links. But now that he'd pieced together a profile of the bomber, as rudimentary as it was, it was clear that he should, and could, make one for their killer, as well.

And something told Stitts that maybe, just maybe, he already had.

"Agent Stitts? Is that all?"

Stitts cleared his throat and blinked several times in rapid succession before continuing.

"The unsub is likely active on these boards, but more as a passive observer and not someone who preaches their own doctrine. I suspect that, as you have suggested, Sgt. Theodore, our suspect will progress until people are injured. And as he becomes more brazen, he will gain confidence, which will be reflected in his social media activity. That's all I can provide you with at this time."

Several hands shot in the air, but Stitts ignored them and hurried out of the room. He walked briskly, aware that Sgt. Theodore was calling after him, but paying him no heed.

As he walked, Stitts pulled his cell phone out of his pocket and dialed Chase's number.

It was a robbery, certainly, but it was also personal. *Very* personal.

Pick up the phone, Chase. Please, pick up the damn phone.

Chapter 38

CHASE PULLED A PAGE out of Stitts's book and just let the grieving mother talk. And Mrs. Hartman was more than willing.

"After my husband died, Mikey was all I had left. And now that he's gone…"

Ms. Hartman sniffed and Chase passed her the small napkin that had come with her scotch. She dabbed her eyes and then took a sip of her martini.

Chase stared at her own drink and contemplated taking a sip. They'd arrived at the bar roughly ten minutes ago, and while during that time Ms. Hartman had polished off her first martini and was halfway through her second, Chase had yet to touch her scotch.

It wasn't because she didn't want to. Lord knows, she *really* wanted to. She also knew that if she took just one sip, it would likely vanquish the last vestiges of the headache that plagued her. But Chase also knew that it was a slippery slope that led to… well, being in bed with a sixty-three-year-old man in the middle of the afternoon, for one.

For the time being, Chase pushed her drink an inch or two toward the center of the table.

"I told… I told Mike that he shouldn't start at the casino, that that was what killed his father. But he wouldn't listen. And with all of the shit that happened… the way the casino was refusing to pay out anything and then the insurance company… He was so angry, and when he saw the bills piling up, he had to get a second job. The Emerald at least let him have that: a job. You see, with my sciatica, I can't work. He was just trying to help us, and he ended up dead, just like his father."

The woman was rambling now, her fatigue amplified by the alcohol, and Chase was having a hard time keeping up. She tried to mentally unpack everything while Ms. Hartman took a sip of her martini and caught her breath.

"Did your husband like his job, Ms. Hartman?"

The woman shrugged.

"At first. But then the smoke got to him. They say he died from a heart attack, but I know it was because of the smoke. Have you been in the casinos? Smoke is everywhere. Oh, they've made some areas non-smoking, but what does that matter? You can't make half a room non-smoking. It goes everywhere. But the private games, they were even worse. That's when they smoke cigars, cigarettes, marijuana, you name it. That's why the insurance company wouldn't pay out, by the way. The marijuana in his system. Harry told me that he put in a formal complaint, but The Emerald said there was no record of it. But I know Harry, he would never, and I mean *never*, smoke drugs."

Chase had to squint in order to keep her eyes from bulging from her head but there was nothing she could do to prevent her jaw from falling open.

It was all there, sitting across from her in the form of a grieving widow: a motive. The complaint, the lack of insurance payout, the negligence on the part of the casino. What had Mike's final Facebook post been?

TRGR: The Rich Get Richer.

Ms. Hartman wiped the tears from her eyes.

"For twenty-seven years Harry worked at The Emerald, first as a waiter then as a croupier—that's the fancy French name for dealer. Eventually, he was a pit boss, but whenever they needed a guy to man the tables, he was there. Then one day, he goes to work and he just... he just died. Massive heart attack. Out of the blue. I mean, he wasn't in the greatest shape, he might have drunk a little too much, and he could've lost a few pounds around the middle, but nobody expected this."

Chase sighed as the woman spoke, trying to put herself in the woman's shoes.

"And how long ago was this, Ms. Hartman?" Chase asked in a soft voice.

Could she, *could Ms. Hartman, be a suspect?*

But why would she kill her own son?

"About six months ago. We—" the woman caught herself. "—I'm still hoping that my appeal comes through and the insurance pays out. Maybe… maybe there's something you can do about that?"

Chase nodded.

"I'll see what I can do, Ms. Hartman."

"Jess, please, just call me Jess."

"Okay, Jess. I just have one question for you: did your son, did Mike have any enemies?"

Ms. Hartman's face sagged. It was clear that speaking about her husband, for whom she'd had time to grieve, had distracted her from her newly deceased son.

"No, he was a nice guy," she sobbed. "Everyone liked him."

Chase slid out of the booth and went over to the woman. She laid a hand on her shoulder and Ms. Hartman immediately collapsed against her. For nearly a full minute, the woman sobbed into her shirt.

If Ms. Hartman—for whatever warped reason—did this, she is one hell of an actor.

Eventually, the woman pulled away.

"I'm okay… I'll be okay," she said, wiping her eyes and nose. "But please, find whoever did this to him, okay? *Please.*"

Chase's eyes fell on the scotch glass.

"Oh, I will. That much I can guarantee. I'll find out whoever did this, and they'll be brought to justice."

Her phone buzzed on the table, and she looked down at it. It was Stitts.

"Ms. Hartman, just one more thing before I have to get back to finding your son's killer."

"Yes?"

"You said Mike had another job. What was it?"

The woman sniffed hard.

"Construction. He was working at the site for the new casino. You know, the one by the airport? The one where they're just breaking ground?"

Chase nodded. She did know the one; it was impossible to miss arriving by airplane, what with all the smoke and procession of dump trucks.

Tomorrow, I'll check it out, she decided. *But right now, I have a poker game to prepare for.*

Chapter 39

STITTS BURST INTO GREG'S office, startling the man so much that his cane clattered to the floor.

"Jesus, you scared the shit out of me," the man said from behind his desk.

"Sorry," Stitts said quickly. "Have you heard from Chase?"

The man's gray eyebrows furrowed.

"No… nor did I expect to."

Stitts shook his head.

"Never mind," he said, making his way over to the board. He started to rearrange the photographs as he spoke. "If you hear from her, please let me know."

"Okay…" Greg replied hesitantly.

"I think… I think that Chase was right all along. This isn't just a robbery, this *is* personal."

Stitts moved all the photos of the victims and everyone else involved in the investigation—including Shane and Peter—to one side. The only person he kept on the right was the photo of Mike Hartman from his casino ID and his mangled body beneath.

"Well, if that's true, I think I just found a motive."

Stitts whipped around.

"What?"

Greg held a single printed page in one hand, and Stitts took it from him.

"My contact came through. Said that the complaint was logged about six months ago, but then was deleted a few days later. Said that he had to dig really deep to find a copy buried in the casino's intranet. Like, *really* deep."

Stitts stared at the paper in his hand. It was a formal complaint issued by employee number 818990: Harry Hartman.

"Speaking of which," Greg continued. "My contact's fee is suddenly blooming out of my pay grade, and considering I don't really have access to the LVMPD petty cash..."

"Chase will take care of it," Stitts replied quickly, not taking his eyes off the paper.

Harry Hartman's complaint was simple and written in his own hand: *Too much smoke during private poker game—cigarettes and weed. Chest hurts, heart palpitations.*

In the spot listing the offending party, Harry had written *Kevin O'Hearn* and *The Emerald*.

Stitts felt his own heart start to race, and when he saw who had signed off on the complaint, it broke into a gallop.

Shane McDuff.

"Shit," he whispered under his breath. Stitts turned back to the board and moved Shane's and Kevin's images over to the same side as Mike's and then hurried back to his desk.

"Everything alright?" Greg asked, but Stitts ignored him.

Rooting through his photos, he found one of the exterior of The Emerald and added it to the board beneath Shane, Kevin, and Mike.

"These were the *real* targets," he said. "The motive."

Greg groaned as he bent to grab his cane, then walked over to Stitts. He reached up and stuck a new picture at the top of the board.

"Then this is our suspect," he said, and both men took a step backward.

Stitts stared up at the board, his upper lip curled. After a moment, he exhaled long and slow and shook his head.

"It still doesn't make sense," he said. Stitts wanted Greg to interject, to tell him that it *did* make sense, that they were finally onto something, but the man let him down.

"Agreed."

Stitts leaned forward and tapped the image of Ms. Hartman at the top of the board.

"Even if we overlook the fact that the statistical likelihood of a woman involved in a shooting of this nature is effectively zero, why in the fuck would she kill and mutilate her own son?"

Greg stayed mum.

"Family strife, maybe? Couldn't be an argument about money, because there was no insurance payout," Stitts continued, thinking out loud now. "And Ms. Hartman was torn up about her son's death, too. *This. Just. Doesn't. Make. Sense.*"

Stitts took out his cell phone and stared at it, hoping that Chase had returned his call.

She hadn't.

Where the hell are you? I could really use your insight right about now.

"My contact also got the video footage that you asked for," Greg said, returning to his desk.

Stitts followed him.

"Geez, maybe your contact is the real Houdini."

Greg chuckled.

"I honestly doubt that."

Stitts knew better than to press a man about his contacts.

"Show me the footage from outside Shane's office around the time of the murders first."

Greg nodded and pulled up a video. It was grainy, but clear enough for Stitts to confirm that it was taken from outside Shane McDuff's office. What surprised him, however, was that he could also see *inside* the office.

For an hour preceding the shootings, Shane's office was empty. People came and went in the hallway, but none of them were of interest to Stitts. Fifteen minutes before the first report of shots fired, Shane appeared in the frame, walking briskly into his office. He sat down at his desk, checked his watch, then picked up the phone.

Several minutes passed, during which time an agitated Shane did nothing more than fiddle with his pen. Four security guards entered the office next, including Mr. Ponytail who had stopped Stitts in the hallway earlier.

"Why did he call them all in before the shooting?" Stitts asked. "That seem strange to you?"

"Just keep watching. It gets even weirder."

Shane said something to the men, to which several of them nodded. The phone appeared to ring then, and Shane picked it up. He said something brief, then hung up.

Stitts glanced at the timestamp.

"That was probably the first call, the complaint about the fireworks going off."

Greg nodded in agreement.

Shane addressed his security once more, but none of them seemed to do much of anything.

Five minutes later, there was a second call. After hanging up this time, Shane said something to Ponytail, who nodded and left the room, presumably to go investigate the complaint.

Greg stopped the tape.

"What the hell," Stitts said. "Shane calls in all of his security and they stay in the office doing pretty much jack shit even after the report of fireworks. It's like... it's like Shane is buying time for the killers to get in and out of the room... however the fuck they managed that."

His eyes darted to the board and he shook his head. Shane was on the *motive* side, not as a suspect.

"Double-crossed, maybe?" Greg offered, reading his mind. "Blackmail?"

Stitts shrugged.

"I have no fucking clue. The only thing I know is that I need to speak to the slimy bastard again."

"Now?"

Stitts shook his head.

"Play the tape a little longer, I want to see footage from the day *after* the shooting."

Greg pressed a few buttons and the video sped forward. Eventually, it showed the police arriving and speaking to Shane as well as various other uninteresting interactions.

"We're running out of tape here," Greg informed him.

Stitts instructed him to keep it going.

Roughly twenty hours after the shooting, a hooded figure appeared at Shane's door. As he reached for it, a frazzled looking Shane emerged. He barked something brief before grabbing the man's arm and heading off-screen.

"Any footage of where they went?" Stitts asked.

Greg shook his head.

"No; and if I were a betting man, I'd put my money on them speaking where Shane knew there were no cameras."

Stitts nodded.

"Go back," he instructed. Greg rewound the tape to where Shane grabbed the man's arm. "No, a little bit more, when the hoodie first reaches for the door. *There*—stop the tape. Now, can you zoom in? Can you zoom in on his hand?"

Greg clicked a few more buttons and the screen magnified. It was even grainer now, but there was enough detail to make out what Stitts wanted to see.

"Well, Ms. Hartman will be happy," Stitts said under his breath.

"Why's that?" Greg asked, squinting at the screen.

Stitts tapped the hooded man's wrist.

"Because, Greg, it looks like we found her son's watch."

Chapter 40

It was a desperate plan, and Chase knew it.

During the entire time that she'd spent with Stu Barnes—the time that Chase could remember, anyway—all he'd spoken about was Kevin. For such a successful businessman, Stu seemed to care little about losing large sums of money. Whether or not he'd be willing to part with two million to back someone he'd only met once, was a different story entirely.

This time when Chase parked in the man's long driveway, she withdrew her badge and gun from the glovebox and slipped them on her person.

It was late, but she knew men like Stu Barnes; they worked into the wee hours of the night and they rose early. This was one of the main contributors to their success. That and being born as an upper-middle-class Caucasian male in the United States of America, of course.

Chase made her way toward the front door, rehearsing what she was going to say in her head. But when the door flew open before she even reached it, Chase was so startled that she forgot her speech.

"Back so soon?" Stu asked. He had changed out of his outfit he was wearing earlier in the day and was now sporting a tailored tracksuit.

"Yeah, about that," Chase said, putting on a fake smile. "We need to talk."

***

"I like you, Chase," Stu said, pouring himself a scotch. He offered Chase one, but she declined. "But my Spidey sense is tingling. Something tells me this is not just a friendly social call."

How astute of you, Chase thought.

"No, it's not. Let me start by apologizing to you; I wasn't completely forthcoming earlier."

As she spoke, Chase pulled her badge out of her pocket, but before she could open it, Stu held up a hand.

"Oh, that's okay. I understand why you didn't want to tell me that you're with the FBI."

Chase's jaw fell slack.

"*You knew?*"

Stu took a sip of his drink and stared at her over the rim of the glass.

"I know a lot about you, Chase Adams," he said. "As soon as I heard about what happened to Kevin, the first thing I did was see who was heading the investigation. But even if I hadn't done that, I would have known that you weren't who you claimed to be. Don't get me wrong, you were good—*damn* good—but you made one mistake."

The man's smugness annoyed her, but Chase decided to play along for now.

"And what's that?"

"You said that Kevin told you about me online. Kevin would never discuss our arrangement, online or otherwise."

Chase chewed her lip, recalling the messages she'd received from *ATM*.

Well, someone out there knows.

She decided to press him further, test his knowledge.

"And do you know why I'm here now?" she asked.

Stu sipped his drink and took his time answering.

"You want to borrow two million dollars," he said simply.

For the second time in as many minutes, Chase was taken by surprise. Stu Barnes was turning out to be a much more interesting character than she'd first thought.

"Two million," Chase repeated.

Stu placed his now empty scotch glass down on the table and stood, turning his back to her.

"You intrigue me, Chase, mostly because you didn't ask me *what* I know about you. Why is that?" Stu said as he made his way toward a large oak desk at the back of the room.

Chase shrugged.

"Why does it matter? Either what you found out about me is a lie, in which case I wouldn't be able to convince you differently, or it's the truth. And if it's the truth, then I already know it."

Stu paused for a second and then chuckled.

"I guess you're right, I've just never heard of someone putting it like that."

He reached under his desk and pulled out a large case and then made his way back towards her.

Chase stared at the case and tried to contain her shock when Stu opened it and showed her stacks upon stacks of neatly wrapped hundred-dollar bills.

She swallowed hard.

And this is why they use chips, because the idea of $2 million in cash is almost incomprehensible.

"You know, there's a good possibility you'll never see this money again," Chase said quietly. "Either I'm going to lose it, be robbed, or, worst of all, it'll be confiscated by the feds."

Stu pushed his lips together and shrugged.

"I'm willing to take that risk, Chase. I'm willing to take that risk because of Kevin. And because of you."

Chase raised an eyebrow and finally managed to pull her eyes away from the money.

"Because of me?"

Stu nodded.

"I've got a lot of money, which affords me a lot of powerful friends. Friends that told me quite a bit about you, Chase. That being said, there are only a few things that really mean anything, that hold any value."

"And what are these *'things*?'" Chase snapped, annoyed at herself for not being able to avoid the trap that she'd so graciously sidestepped earlier.

"That you're a closer, Chase. Everything you get involved in, for good or for worse, comes to an end. It happened in Alaska, it happened in Boston, and it happened in Chicago. And I know you'll do whatever it takes to find out who killed my friend Kevin O'Hearn."

Chapter 41

"You didn't seriously wake me up in the middle of the night and haul my ass in here for this, did you?"

Stitts stared at the sergeant. Fully dressed in his uniform, it was clear that Sgt. Theodore hadn't left the office yet, but Stitts let this slide.

"Ms. Hartman claims that her son would never go anywhere without his watch. And we know from his Facebook photos that he's always wearing it."

Sgt. Theodore frowned.

"That's it? That's all you got? A shady manager who meets with a guy—who you can't identify, by the way—who's wearing a watch that *looks* like the watch of one of the deceased? Seriously?"

Stitts couldn't help but feel that what he'd presented was underwhelming when stated so succinctly.

Sgt. Theodore squinted at the printout.

"How can you even tell that it's the same watch? It just looks like a shitty Timex to me."

Stitts couldn't argue with that. He handed over the complaint made by Harry Hartman next.

"What about the shady manager? The complaint made by Mike's father?"

"This is Vegas, son. Everyone either looks or is shady.

Stitts was getting desperate now.

"But it all adds up to a motive."

"A motive for *who*? If you tell me Ms. Hartman, I'm going to send you on a direct flight back to Quantico, Stitts."

Stitts ground his teeth and said nothing.

"The motive is money," the sergeant continued. "Always is, always was."

He calmly folded his hands together and laid them on the desk.

"Look, I called you in on this job because I thought you guys could help. I *still* think you can help. But I'm stretched to my limits here. After the Planned Parenthood and Gay Jesus church bombings, I've got all my men out there in the field looking for some guy—some guy who you said in your profile was going to escalate. I've got men stationed throughout the entire city at any possible location that has anything to do with gays or drag queens or abortions—*anything*. I just don't have the manpower to help you out right now. It's not that I don't care about the victims, I do. But I have a public safety issue at hand that takes precedence. I hope you can understand that."

I understand that you know solving which crime will help you get promoted, Stitts thought. *That's what I understand.*

"I gave you Greg, but that's all I can offer right now."

You gave me Greg, and as helpful as he's been, you only did that because no one else wants to work with the man.

"With all due respect, Sgt. Theodore, I've got eleven dead bodies—"

Sgt. Theodore flexed his jaw before interrupting.

"With all due respect to *you*, Agent Stitts, *you* don't have *any* dead bodies. The shooting occurred on Las Vegas soil, which means that they are *my* dead bodies. Let's keep in mind that I asked you to come in and help, not the other way around. I can just as easily send you back home."

Stitts felt anger build up inside him.

"That's right, you asked the FBI to help, only you tie my hands once I get here. Doesn't make sense. There's someone out there—"

"You want me to tell you what I think happened? I think that some ex-military group found out about the game, came in, grabbed the cash, and ran. One of the security guards probably took a shot at them, so they took him out. And once one was dead, it only made sense to kill them all. It's already felony murder, so why leave potential witnesses behind?"

Stitts gawked at the man. His simplistic reasoning was so flawed that it was almost comical.

"Are you serious?"

Something inside Sgt. Theodore's face broke then, and Stitts realized that they were playing their own poker game. Only the stakes weren't cash, but people's lives.

"Stitts, I'm sorry, but there's so much political pressure to solve these bombings, that you wouldn't believe it. Let me find this asshole, then I'll give you all the resources I have at my disposal. For right now, however, I just can't do it."

Stitts stood, looked at Greg beside him, and then gestured towards the door.

"Stitts, you're not to bring anybody in, not now. Just follow the manager if you think he's involved, build intel, and when this mess is over, I'll help. I swear."

Yeah, I need your help like I need a hole in my head.

Eleven people dead and all he cares about is some broken windows. What in the hell is this world coming to?

I'm just going to have to take things into my own hands.

PART III – Reformation

PRESENT DAY

Chapter 42

CHAOS.

Just as the dealer dealt the flop—Q, 6, Q—the entire room erupted into chaos.

First, the hotel door blew inward, and then the bullets started to fly. One of the security guards was taken by surprise and was hit in the shoulder and chest. He went down without firing a shot.

The other guard was more prepared. He slipped the pistol from his jacket and leaped to one side.

Aside from Chase and the second guard, no one else in the room reacted; it was as if they were frozen in time. She saw Mike Darwish eat a bullet in the leg and as he bent over, another tore through his neck. Blood spurted onto the table, soaking his cash and the felt.

Both Tim Tigner and *The Guru* were struck at the same time, although Chase couldn't tell exactly where, given that she had slipped to the floor the second the door exploded.

All of this happened in a matter of seconds, and yet there were already rivers of blood soaking the carpet. Someone yelled—maybe Chase, maybe the attacker—and the dealer finally reacted.

He flipped the table forward, sending cards and cash flying into the air. Several rounds easily passed through the wood and the dealer's white shirt suddenly bloomed with red.

The rich divorcee, Deb Koch, collapsed next to Chase and she instinctively pulled the woman close, trying to protect her from stray bullets that still rained above them.

"Stay down," Chase whispered, wishing that she'd chanced bringing her gun to the game even though it would have almost certainly been confiscated at the door.

When the woman didn't reply, Chase leaned back an inch. Deb's glassy eyes stared at her.

Chase's initial instinct was to shove the woman's dead body away, but at the last second, she thought better of it. Instead, she pulled Deb on top of her and then wedged her body against the base of the overturned poker table.

Gunfire continued to fill the room, but now she heard the sound of an alarm or siren from somewhere in the hallway.

Chase tried to catch her bearings, to determine how many attackers there were, but from her vantage point, she could only see the security guard. He was to her left, near the wall of windows, lying on his side. He'd been struck in the leg at least once, but this didn't seem to slow him down.

As she watched, the man squeezed off several more rounds, his face twisted in concentration.

Chase observed with gritted teeth, wanting to spring to her feet and do… *something*.

But to do so would mean certain death; she was helpless.

A grunt came from the other side of the table and, based on the change in the security guard's face, Chase knew that at least one of the assailants had been struck. The guard started to rise to his feet, dragging his wounded leg behind him, when something strange happened.

The pressure in the room changed.

It took Chase a few moments to realize what was happening, and then she started to yell.

"Behind you!" she screamed. "Behind you! *Look out!*"

Chapter 43

"**We should get some** sleep," Stitts said, rubbing his eyes. He checked his watch. It was nearly four in the morning.

Greg leaned out from behind his monitor.

"You might want to take a look at this first," he said.

Stitts yawned and made his way over.

"What is it?"

"Another video… the one you asked for, tracking the food service cart."

"Alright," Stitts said. "Let's watch it then pack it in for the night… or morning."

Greg nodded and fired up the video. It was actually a composite of several videos from different cameras around the casino all stitched together rather seamlessly.

Stitts made a mental note for Chase to give whoever Greg's contact was a significant bonus. The man got shit done.

The first video was taken from a loading dock and showed the waiter, Peter Doherty, standing on the edge, smoking a cigarette. Greg sped up the tape and they watched the man pace for nearly fifteen minutes before a box truck appeared. Peter guided the truck in, then the rear door was rolled up. There was someone in the back of the truck, but based on the shadow cast by the interior, Stitts couldn't make out who. Together, Peter and the man struggled to pull a large black bag out and drag it onto the loading dock. It was heavy, and Peter's face strained with the effort. The two men exchanged words, then the truck pulled away again.

When the truck was out of sight, Peter set about the difficult task of stuffing the bag beneath the food service cart.

"So there *was* something hidden under there," Greg said absently.

On screen, Peter laid the white tablecloth over the top of the cart, then smoothed the sides. Confident that there were no unsightly bulges, he nodded seemingly to himself, and then pushed the cart back inside. The video then switched to a much brighter view of the inside of the kitchen. After saying something to several waiters, Peter grabbed a plate with the burger and fries and put it on the cart. After covering the food with a silver cloche, he moved forward. The video then switched to him getting into the elevator, then exiting on the seventh floor.

They'd already seen the rest.

"What the hell is in the bag?" Greg muttered.

Stitts chewed the inside of his lip.

"Go back to the video outside the loading dock," he instructed.

Something wasn't adding up.

Greg played the video at half speed and when the bag flopped partway onto the loading dock, Peter grabbed what looked like a handle.

"There," Stitts said, pointing at the handle. "Do you think you can zoom in on that just a little?"

Greg did, and Stitts inhaled sharply.

"What in the hell?"

There wasn't one handle on the bag, but eight; four on either side, evenly spaced.

"You ever seen handles like that on a bag before?" he asked.

"Yeah," Greg answered, swallowing hard. "At the Village shooting—many of them."

"Me too," Stitts almost whispered. "It's a goddamn body bag."

Silence fell over the room for several seconds before Stitts piped up again.

"You know how I said that maybe there was a body under the cart?"

Greg turned to face him now, a serious expression on his face.

"Well, there was. Only it was a *dead* body."

Greg's eyebrows knitted again.

"But… why? And where did it go?" he sighed. "What the fuck, man. I'm too tired for this. I don't understand—"

"Can you go back again?" Stitts asked, ignoring Greg's comments. "I want to see if we can figure out who's in the back of the truck."

Greg rewound the video and they watched it several times before Stitts shook his head.

"Impossible. It's all just shadows. But—"

Stitts grabbed the mouse and jogged the video back and forth. Just when the men pulled the body bag onto the loading dock, a car must have entered the parking lot. Headlights lit up the back of the truck and, even though they never touched the man's face, they reflected off something leaning up against the interior wall.

"Oh, fuuuuccccck," Stitts moaned.

Everything suddenly clicked into place.

His own words came back to him, the ones that he'd said to Sgt. Theodore in the hallway on the way to give his profile.

We've got dead bodies and all you have is broken glass.

There was also the second call, the one about the sound of breaking glass to Shane McDuff. The one that he'd assumed was from the bottles behind the bar smashing.

Only he was wrong.

Dead wrong.

His mind flashed to earlier in the evening, when he'd rapped his knuckles off the seventh-floor windows. They'd been perfect. *Too* perfect.

And now he knew why.

"What? What is it?" Greg asked.

Stitts ignored him again and walked over to the board. He tore down Ms. Hartman's photo and moved Mike Hartman's image in her place.

"What? You think a dead man did all this?" Greg asked.

"No, not a dead man," Stitts replied, staring at Mike's face. "But someone we were supposed to think was dead."

Chapter 44

THE SECURITY GUARD HESITATED, clearly trying to figure out where the voice was coming from given that Chase was mostly buried beneath Deb Koch's corpse.

And this moment of indecision cost the man his life.

The window behind him exploded inward, sending a rush of air into the room. In the darkness, Chase picked out the outline of a person, only they appeared to be levitating *outside* the fourteenth-floor window. Before Chase could wrap her mind around how this was possible, her vision flashed with muzzle fire. The security guard went down and this time, he didn't get back up.

"Mike! Mike, we need to get the fuck out of here!" the hovering figure shouted.

Chase's body seized. She wanted nothing more than to stand and confront these assholes, put a bullet in their foreheads.

But getting herself killed would mean letting down Ms. Hartman and Stu Barnes. And Chase had let enough people down for one day, one week, a lifetime.

As slowly and carefully as possible, Chase teased Deb's body on top of her until only one of her eyes remained visible.

"Forget the money!" the man shouted from the window. "We need to get the fuck out of here, man!"

"They owe me," Mike spat back through clenched teeth. "These assholes owe me!"

As he shoved stacks of bills into a bag, Chase focused on his hand, his wrist. His *watch*.

A very specific watch. Not expensive by any means, but one that Chase recognized.

It was the watch that Mrs. Hartman had showed her. It was the watch that Mike Hartman never left the house without.

What the fuck?

"Come on!"

In addition to the fire alarm, the room was suddenly filled with a metallic ratcheting sound as the man in the window started to lower out of sight.

With a curse, Mike sprinted across the room toward the smashed window. He had been hit once, Chase saw, maybe even twice, judging by the dark stain on his shoulder.

Just before he leaped out of the window, the man turned back and their eyes met.

It was a fleeting glance, one that lasted no more than a fraction of a second. But Chase still knew, without a doubt, who the murderer was.

I was almost killed by a dead man, Chase thought moments before she passed out. *I was almost killed by Mike Hartman.*

Chapter 45

STITTS THREW THE DOOR to Shane McDuff's office open so violently that it nearly closed again before Greg could follow him inside.

Shane was so startled that he almost fell out of his chair.

"What—what are you—"

Stitts strode across the room and hovered over the cowering man.

"Surprised to see you here this late," Stitts snapped. "What, can't sleep? Something on your mind? On your conscience?"

"You can't—you can't—"

"Show me your fucking arms, Shane."

When the man didn't answer, Stitts grabbed his wrist and yanked up his sleeve.

Shane's arm was adorned with dozens of tattoos, all of varying quality, mostly shitty.

Stitts backed away, a disgusted look on his face.

"You like to do your own tattoos, don't you, Shane? And let me guess, your best work was a sparrow, am I right?"

"Yeah… so-so what. That's not a crime."

"No, no it's not. But tattooing a corpse? That is. Isn't it, Greg?"

The officer, who was standing in the doorway and effectively blocking the view of the cameras from the hall, nodded.

"Desecration of a human corpse is indeed a crime."

"That's right," Stitts said.

"I don't know what you're talking about. I think… I think I need a lawyer." Shane reached for the phone, but Stitts slammed his hand down on top of it.

"You don't know what I'm talking about? Hmm? Well, let me ask you this, then: do you know how much one of the windows in this hotel weighs?"

"Wha-wha-what?"

"The windows, Shane. How much do they weigh?"

"I don't—"

"A little? A lot? Oh, they're pretty big; I bet they weigh a lot. I bet they weigh so much that it would take a while for your buddy Peter Doherty to replace them on the seventh floor. But fake windows, temporary windows… they could go up pretty quick, am I right? Like maybe just a few minutes, if you knew what you were doing? What do you think, Shane?"

Shane looked like he was either going to cry or crap his pants—maybe both.

"That's why he had to come back the day *after* the shooting. Peter had to take his time to replace the fake windows he put up with the *real* ones before anyone noticed that they were different."

"I don't—I just—I—"

"*Eleven people are dead, Shane! Eleven people were murdered up there!*" Stitts shouted.

Tears streamed down Shane's cheeks now and his face turned a deep scarlet.

"No one was supposed to die!" Shane yelled back. "*No one was supposed to die!*"

Stitts snarled.

"Oh, but they did, Shane, and that makes you an accomplice to murder. Hey, Greg, we have the death penalty in Nevada, don't we?"

"We do."

Shane started to sob now.

"I didn't want anyone to get hurt!" he exclaimed.

"Death penalty, Shane. You better start talking or I'll petition for lethal injection."

With tears spilling down his cheeks, Shane started to open up.

"They told me to tear up the complaint after Harry Hartman died, that if I didn't do it, then they would fire me."

"Who did, Shane? Who told you to tear up the complaint?"

"The casino… my boss… I dunno!"

"But Harry's son… Mike… he knew about it, didn't he?"

"Yes," Shane shouted back. "He said he had a copy and that he was going to sue the casino. Said I was going to be charged with tampering with evidence or some shit! He just… he said he was just going to rob the players, take their money. I didn't think anyone would get hurt, let alone die…"

The phone on his desk rang and Shane jumped.

Stitts's first instinct was to tell the man to leave it, but for some reason, he changed his mind.

"Pick it up," he ordered. With a trembling hand, Shane grabbed the receiver and brought to his ear.

"Shane McDuff," he blubbered.

The man had been pale ever since Stitts had entered the room, but now he went completely white.

"No," Shane moaned. The phone slipped from his hand and clattered on the desk.

"What is it?" Stitts demanded. When Shane didn't answer, he grabbed the phone.

"Hello? Hello?"

The line was dead.

"Shane, who the fuck was that? Shane, you better—"

The man's eyes suddenly lifted and locked on Stitts's.

"There's been another shooting," he said in an airy whisper. "It happened again."

Chapter 46

CHASE OPENED HER EYES and confusion washed over her. There was blood everywhere—on her face, her hands, her arms.

It took her several seconds to figure out where she was and when she did, her first instinct was to rise to her feet. But then she heard voices and froze again.

"Look what you did! This is you, Shane! *This is all your fault!*"

"Oh my god," someone moaned, followed by a wail.

"You did this!"

This last voice was one she recognized; it belonged to someone she was very familiar with.

Chase grunted and slid Deb's corpse off her. Then she somehow managed to convince her stiff and sore body to rise.

Even though one of her eyes was stuck together with blood, Chase still saw enough for her guts to flip.

The scene was like the seventh-floor massacre, only because she'd been part of this one, it seemed even more visceral.

All of the poker players were dead, their bodies strewn across the floor like discarded waste. There were bundles of cash everywhere, and everything—the walls, the floor, the cards—was sprayed with blood.

Her chest hitched and she wiped at her eyes.

In the doorway stood Jeremy Stitts, his gun leveled at her chest. There was a man on his knees in front of him, but his face was buried in his hands and Chase couldn't tell who it was. Behind Stitts were several police officers that struggled to get into the room.

When their eyes met, Stitts's face seemed to collapse inward.

"Chase? Chase—what the fuck?"

Stitts lowered his gun and then dropped it completely and ran to her.

"Are you okay?" he asked, gripping her sides gently and feeling her entire body.

Chase didn't—*couldn't*—answer right away. She'd been shot once before, right through the hip by Agent Martinez, and that had hurt like hell. But she recalled that after the initial pain, the wound had gone numb as adrenaline flooded her system. At present, she didn't *feel* like she'd been shot, but that didn't mean she hadn't been.

"Jesus Christ, Chase, what are you doing here?" Stitts asked as he continued to search her body.

"I… I think I'm okay," she said quietly. A quick, internal rundown of her body revealed that aside from a small throbbing pain on her hairline, she couldn't identify any other injuries. Chase brought a hand up and delicately touched her forehead. It wasn't a bullet hole, thank God, but a gash. She must have struck her head on the table on the way down. It felt deep, and it was undoubtedly the reason for the blood in her eye, but she didn't think it was serious.

Now, after confirming that she was okay, she suddenly collapsed into Stitts's arms.

"Oh god," she moaned as he held her.

More men entered the room now, several of whom immediately exited again to retch in the hallway. Others eyed Stitts and Chase with confused expressions on their faces.

"What the fuck happened, Chase? What are you doing here?" Stitts sobbed.

Chase could barely catch her breath, let alone answer. Every time she closed her eyes, she pictured the spray of bullets, Deb's face, the security guard as he was mowed down by the figure in the window.

"You're bleeding," Stitts said at last. He removed a wad of tissue from his pocket and dotted the top of her head. Chase, managing to collect herself somewhat, took it from him and held it to the wound herself.

"I'm okay, Stitts," she said with a swallow. "I think... I think I'm all right."

There was an audible gasp from Chase's right, which drew everyone's attention.

The dealer lay on his back, blood trickling from the corners of his mouth. He had been shot in the chest several times, but by some miracle still appeared to be breathing.

"Get an ambulance in here!" Stitts shouted. "They're still alive! Oh god, they're still alive in here!"

Chapter 47

SO MUCH HAPPENED IN rapid succession—the panes of glass in the box truck, Shane's confession, the shooting—that Stitts's mind had a difficult time piecing them together in a chronological order.

And Chase... Chase was here. Somehow, Chase was *here*.

The only thing that kept him sane was the fact that she was okay. There was a cut on her forehead that would likely require stitches, but by some miracle, she'd escaped the carnage that had taken everyone else's lives.

They were in the hallway now, trying to stay out of the way of the paramedics and police officers that stormed the scene. Even though several minutes had passed since coming to the fourteenth floor, Stitts's heart would not stop racing in his chest. It was thudding so fast and so powerfully that it affected his speech.

"What the hell... what the hell are you doing here, Chase?"

From somewhere in the room, a paramedic announced that the dealer had since died. Shane, who was handcuffed to a the door, sobbed loudly.

Gauze still pressed to her head, Chase's chest hitched before answering.

"I... I was just trying to..."

She couldn't even finish the sentence. Chase's legs buckled and Stitts only just managed to catch her before she fell to the floor.

Her body trembled like a plucked violin string in his arms, and Stitts squeezed her tight.

I'll hold you like this forever, he thought incomprehensibly. *I'll hold you for as long as you want, Chase.*

But it didn't last forever.

"Jesus Christ, Stitts, what the hell happened?"

Stitts raised his eyes to see Greg coming out of the elevator, leaning heavily on his cane as he approached. His eyes flicked to Shane on the floor, to the woman in his arms.

"It's Chase," Stitts said as if that were a sufficient explanation for the madness he'd witnessed.

Greg's face went pale.

"Jesus, is she okay?"

In his arms, Chase quaked once more, but then she pushed herself away from Stitts's chest.

"I'm okay," she said softly. "I'll be okay."

But to Stitts, she looked anything but okay. In fact, she looked much like she had when Stitts had approached her back at Grassroots Recovery: bleary-eyed and frightened.

It was too soon… everything happened too soon.

It had been a horrible mistake bringing her to Las Vegas, he realized. A terrible, disastrous mistake.

"Chase, what were you—"

This time Greg was cut off by the elevator opening.

Sgt. Theodore strode toward them, his face red.

"What in the fuck happened here?" he demanded. When he saw the bloody gauze on Chase's forehead, his upper lip curled in confusion. "What the hell?"

The man paused mid-step and he looked to Stitts for an explanation.

"Agent Stitts, what is going on?" he demanded.

But it wasn't Stitts who answered. It was Chase.

"The killer struck again—just like we said he would. And now maybe you'll get off your ass and stop looking for a man who blows up doorways and start hunting for a real killer."

Chapter 48

TO CHASE'S UTTER DISBELIEF, even after everything that had happened, including Shane's confession, Sgt. Theodore was still reluctant to admit that their unsub was Mike Hartman.

Someone who *looked* like Mike, sure, but not *the* Mike Hartman.

"I felt the corpse's arm," Chase said. "It was recently shaved, because Shane just tattooed him. The real Mike got his tattoo years ago."

"Maybe he just likes to shave his arms," Sgt. Theodore shot back. "Did you consider that?"

"And it's just a coincidence that the corpse's fingers were cut up with glass so that we can't run his prints. The fact is, the body in that room is a plant... I have no idea who it is, but it most definitely isn't Mike Hartman?"

Sgt. Theodore sighed.

"This fingerprint issue seemed suspicious only *after* you convinced yourself that it wasn't Mike Hartman's body, not before. Not when you first arrived on the scene."

Chase threw her arms in the air.

"This is fucking ridiculous. I *saw* him. I saw Mike with a goddamn AR-15 strapped to his chest."

The sergeant shook his head.

"You *think* you saw Mike Hartman while bullets were flying overhead and you had blood and bodies everywhere."

"I know—"

Sgt. Theodore held up a hand, halting her mid-sentence.

"What does it matter anyway? I've put an APB out for someone who looks like Mike Hartman—and if he's been hit in the shoulder like you say, he's going to turn up at a hospital somewhere—why does it matter if it's him or someone else?"

Chase felt her blood start to boil and was about to lash out when Stitts calmed her with a hand on her shoulder.

"It matters because this isn't just about poker players, Sergeant. This is about revenge. We think that Mike has something bigger planned."

"Yeah? Like what?" Sergeant Theodore barked. It was clear that the man was nearing his wit's end. The problem was, Chase had already long since passed the point of no return.

"Like *what*? Is murdering eighteen people not enough? Who knows, maybe he'll bomb—"

She stopped mid-sentence, her heart racing.

"You said Mike had another job. What was it?"

"Construction. He was working at the site for the new casino. You know, the one by the airport? The one where they're just breaking ground?"

"What?" Stitts asked, once again laying a hand on her shoulder. "Are you okay?"

Chase shrugged him off.

"Mike worked in construction for the new casino," she said quietly. "The one that they're breaking ground for by the airport. The one that they're using TNT to blast the rock."

"That's it," Sgt. Theodore said, rising to his feet. "If you're going to tell me that the bombings and the shootings are related, I'm going—"

"It makes sense!" Chase exclaimed. "The bombings happened immediately after the shootings—"

"That's enough!" the sergeant hollered.

"—and they are the perfect distraction—"

"Enough!"

Stitts grabbed her arm, but she shook free.

"—and explains why no one was hurt, because Mike—"

"*Enough!*"

"—doesn't have anything against them. It's just—"

"That's it," the now purple-faced sergeant yelled. "You two are off the case."

"You can't do that," Chase shot back.

"The fuck I can't." Sgt. Theodore snapped his fingers and the door to his office suddenly opened.

Chase looked skyward as Josh Haskell poked his head in.

"Yup?"

"The FBI was just saying that they think the shootings and bombings are related, which—"

"Seriously?" Josh asked.

"—which means that now the DoD is taking the lead. Team up with ATF and get started right away."

Josh nodded, the pink wattles beneath his chin quivering.

"Right away, boss."

When he was gone, the sergeant had the gall to smile.

"See? You're off the case."

Chase rose to her feet.

"Fuck you," she spat. "Fuck you, you fucking—"

Stitts grabbed her arm and this time his grip was such that she was unable to shake him off.

"Chase, c'mon."

"You can take us off the case, but I'm not going anywhere. I'm staying in Las Vegas and seeing this thing through."

"Chase, please."

She was acutely aware that Stitts was guiding her toward the door now.

"Buh-bye," Sgt. Theodore said with a sarcastic wave.

Chase gave him the finger and let Stitts escort her from the room.

Chapter 49

"THIS IS COMPLETE AND utter bullshit," Stitts said as he and Chase made their way down the hallway toward Greg's office.

"That's my line," Chase grumbled. Now that she was no longer staring at Sgt. Theodore's smug face, her blood pressure had normalized somewhat. "But look, it doesn't matter. We haven't needed Sgt. Theodore or any of them from the start, and we don't need them now."

Stitts nodded in agreement.

"You really think that Mike could be behind the bombings as well?"

Chase chewed her lip and thought about it for a moment. In the sergeant's office, the idea had struck her like a lightning bolt and she'd been absolutely certain. Now, no longer in the heat of the moment, she was less convinced.

"Yes... maybe. I mean, it *does* make sense—it's the perfect distraction."

"But why not do some real damage, then? Injure or hurt some people? That would raise even more flags and attention, and clearly Mike is not opposed to murder," Stitts said, falling into his normal routine as the Devil's Advocate.

"True, but he's got nothing against Planned Parenthood or the church. His vendetta is with the casino."

"And Kevin O'Hearn."

Chase stopped walking and she turned to face Stitts.

"What do you mean?"

"Kevin was listed in the complaint that Mike's father made. He was the one smoking the weed, which ultimately resulted in the insurance company and the casino backing out of any payout."

Chase thought briefly of Stu Barnes and how close he was with Kevin.

"Shit," she whispered. "That's why he killed them. He blamed the casino *and* the poker players for his father's death."

"Sure seems that way," Stitts replied. He knocked on the window of Greg's office and, when the man looked up, he gestured for him to join them.

"And let me guess, Shane McDuff was in charge when Harry worked at the casino?"

"Not only that, but he signed Harry's complaint. *And* he tore it up after Harry died, allegedly at the behest of the casino brass. That was the leverage Mike used to get Shane involved."

The final pieces were all falling into place now.

"And he probably knew that Shane would crack under pressure and incriminate himself. That's how he was getting back at Shane," Chase said.

"What about Peter and Tony? The window washer and the waiter?"

"He needed them to get away clean… probably just convinced them with a big payday. No one has seen the waiter since the first shooting," Chase said as Greg joined them in the hallway. "And I bet Peter was the man I saw in the broken window on the fourteenth floor."

"Probably," Stitts concurred.

"Hey, guys?" Greg said, a concerned look on his face.

"Yeah?" Stitts asked.

"Sgt. Theodore just gave me a ring, said I'm to put all my energy into helping the ATF and DoD. Something about the cases being connected?"

Chase glared at the man.

"And?"

"And fuck that guy. He's an asshole. Where're we headed?"

Chase chuckled. Despite everything, she somehow managed to find some humor in what Greg had just said.

Sgt. Theodore *was* an asshole.

"There's someone that I think we should talk to again," Chase said.

"Yeah? And who's that?" Stitts asked as they neared the front of the station.

Stitts's tone surprised Chase. Back in the hotel, he'd been relieved that she was okay. Back in Sgt. Theodore's office, he'd had her back. But now that they were on their own again, with only Greg as support, it was clear that he was pissed at her. And he had every right to be after she'd taken off again and almost gotten herself killed.

But Stitts's feelings would have to wait. There were more pressing matters to attend to.

"Mike's mother, that's who," Chase said as they burst through the doors and into the morning light.

Chapter 50

"ARE YOU GONNA TELL her about her son?" Greg asked from the backseat. When they left the station, they'd opted for Stitts's rental, which was less conspicuous than Greg's squad car. Together, the three of them drove to the bar where Chase had met Ms. Hartman the day prior, and where they'd planned to meet again.

"I don't... I don't know," Chase said. "I'm not entirely sure if she's involved or not, to be honest. I don't think so, but it wouldn't be impossible."

"Well, I don't like it," Stitts offered. This was a predictable response from the man, but Chase bit her tongue. "If she is involved, who's to say that Mike won't arrive to finish the job? After all, you're the only one who saw him. What if Ms. Hartman only agreed to the meeting so that Mike could take out the only living witness to his crimes?"

Chase shook her head. Mike Hartman had come into the room guns a-blazing, knowing that there were two highly trained security guards present. Sure, he had the element of surprise on his side, and support from Peter Doherty, but it wasn't organized and calculated like the first attack. This one had been a spur-of-the-moment attack, a final fuck you to the poker community and the players before the main event.

Whatever that was.

"You could stand guard—the both of you. If anything goes wrong, I'll look to you, my protectors, to save me."

Stitts grimaced.

"You've got a real fucking suicidal streak in you, don't you, Chase?"

The smile slid off Chase's face. The comment had hit too close to home, and it still stung her deeply.

All of a sudden, she could taste Louisa's fat fingers in her throat, the dry methadone pills working their way back up her esophagus.

"Fuck you, Stitts."

With that, she opened her door and stepped out of the car.

"You guys are like a married couple, you know that?" Chase heard Greg say from inside the car.

Still fuming, Chase didn't wait for Stitts's reply.

For a one o'clock in the afternoon on a Saturday in Vegas, the bar was surprisingly empty. Ms. Hartman, one of the few patrons, sat in a booth near the back.

To her surprise, Ms. Hartman scowled as Chase slid into the booth across from her.

"Care to tell me what this is all about?" Ms. Hartman spat. She looked as if she hadn't slept since the last time they'd met. For what it was worth, Chase hadn't either.

"Excuse me?"

The woman shoved a black bag reminiscent of an old-school medical case across the table at Chase. It jarred her elbow, but Chase didn't take her eyes off the woman in case this was just meant as a distraction.

"Open it," Ms. Hartman instructed.

Chase didn't bite. With the bombs now likely linked to Mike Hartman and his crew, she wasn't too keen on opening suspicious packages.

"You open it," Chase countered.

The woman pursed her lips, and for a brief second Chase thought that she would decline the offer. But then Ms. Hartman reached over, unzipped the bag, and opened it wide.

Only then did Chase allow her eyes to drift from the woman's face and focus on the bag's contents. Then she immediately looked back up again.

"Where did you get this from?" Chase asked.

Ms. Hartman frowned.

"Someone left it on my doorstep. I really, really need to know what the hell is going on, Chase," she said, her tone suddenly softening.

Chase's eyes darted back to the bag and she did some quick mental math. Although the bar was dark, the familiar ten-thousand-dollar bands wrapped around bundles of cash were easily identifiable. If she had to guess, Chase would have pegged the amount at around five- or six-hundred-thousand dollars.

She was positive that Ms. Hartman wasn't involved now, just as she was certain that it was her son who had left her the cash. And yet, Chase was undecided if she should tell the woman about Mike, mostly because she didn't know if he was still going to be alive by the end of the day.

"There was also this," Ms. Hartman said, pulling a folded piece of paper from her pocket and putting it on the table between them.

There were three typed lines on the small section of paper that read:

Prick forth the airy knights, and couch their spears,
Till thickest legions close; with feats of arms
From either end of heaven the welkin burns.

Chase read the lines several times, trying to make sense of the poem. They meant nothing to her.

"What... what does it mean?" she asked, reaching for the paper.

Ms. Hartman snatched it back and put it in her pocket.

"I don't know... I don't know what any of this means," Ms. Hartman said softly.

Silence fell over the two of them for a moment, their eyes locked, and Chase couldn't help but feel for the woman.

Like Ms. Hartman, Chase's own husband and son had abandoned her. While the circumstances differed vastly, the similarities were undeniable.

There was also the case of the three empty martini glasses by Ms. Hartman's elbow. She could relate to that, too.

Chase took a deep breath and then dabbed at her forehead, which was still bleeding a little despite the glue that the paramedic had applied to the cut on her hairline.

"Ms. Hartman, there's something you should know and something I think you should do. But first, you have to tell me something about your son, about Mike."

Chapter 51

STITTS WATCHED THE EXCHANGE between Ms. Hartman and his partner at a distance. The woman was showing Chase something inside a bag, but from his vantage point at the bar, Stitts couldn't make it out. Their discussion transitioned from angry to sad. And then something in Ms. Hartman's face broke, but when Chase reached across to comfort her, the woman recoiled.

He heard his partner say that she was sorry, and for a second, Stitts thought tears might have appeared in Chase's eyes as well. Then she pushed the bag back across the table to Ms. Hartman and made her way toward the door. As Chase passed Stitts, she grumbled that he should come with her under her breath.

Stitts casually finished his beer, left a ten on the counter, and then hurried after Chase.

Once outside, he was bombarded by a strange noise, something that sounded oddly like drums, but when he looked around, Stitts couldn't see anything.

"What happened?" he asked, struggling to catch up to his partner.

Chase discretely wiped her eyes, clearly hoping that Stitts wouldn't notice.

He did.

"She's not involved," Chase said. "Ms. Hartman has no idea that her son is still alive."

They were almost at the car when Stitts grabbed her by the shoulder and spun her around.

"What did she say, Chase? What the hell is going on?"

Stitts had it up to his eyeballs with all the secretive crap. It was nearly laughable that his main argument with Director

Hampton to get Chase reinstated was that he needed a partner who he could trust, who would have his back. In truth, not only could he not trust Chase, but Stitts was no longer certain that if push came to shove, he wouldn't be a bird on a wire.

His mind unexpectedly drifted to his mother then, lying in a hospital bed, likely all alone, and he felt a pang of guilt. He'd been so wrapped up in this case, so completely preoccupied with either trying to find Chase or to follow her around, that he'd completely forgotten about her.

The poor woman had suffered a stroke and her only son didn't even know if she was still alive.

Stitts felt his own lids tingle and it took all his willpower to force his tears away. He would deal with his mother later, but right now, he had to catch a killer.

"Tell me, Chase. For God's sake, tell me what the hell is going on."

Chapter 52

"TRGR," Chase said at last, staring Stitts in the eyes. She could tell that the man was frustrated, but Chase wasn't sure how to express what she felt.

It was like the first time that she'd been transported into the eyes of the dead. How could you tell a person that without them thinking you were insane?

"What?"

"The Rich Get Richer; Mike Hartman's not done yet. He wants to strike a dagger in the heart of the company that fucked him and his family."

Chase opened the car door then and lowered herself behind the wheel. Stitts got into the front seat and Greg, who she presumed had been at the bar despite not seeing him, reappeared and got in the back.

Chase put the car into drive and started out of the parking lot. They had barely made it a quarter block before the traffic came to a complete standstill.

"Chase, tell me what she said," Stitts implored. "What was in the bag?"

With a sigh, Chase finally answered the man.

"She had... she had a bag of money. Ms. Hartman had no idea where it came from, but it was from him; Mike left it for her."

Stitts's brow knitted.

"And you're sure she's not involved?"

"I'm sure," Chase replied, leaning on the horn. All of a sudden, she didn't feel like talking about this anymore.

"But how?" Stitts pressed. "How can you be so sure?"

"I just am."

"Chase..."

Chase turned to face Stitts, her eyes blazing.

"I just know, okay? The woman just lost her husband and son… there's no way you can fake that shit. Trust me, I know."

Stitts looked like he was going to say something more, and Chase waited, teeth clenched. Eventually, he broke the stare.

Feeling her temperature rise, Chase rolled down her window. A drumroll suddenly filled the car.

The cool air served to dissipate some of her anger and frustration.

"I don't think he's done… there was a note, some weird poem. I think… I think Mike is going to blow up the casino," she said quietly.

"Yeah, I don't mean to interrupt, but that's going to be next to impossible," Greg said from the backseat. "Security is way too tight at The Emerald. Besides, there's an APB out on Mike, and if he shows up at The Emerald, he's going to be dragged away in chains. Sgt. Theodore may be a complete asshole, but he's not an absolute moron. Despite everything he told you guys, I know for a fact that he has several teams staking out the place."

Chase sighed again.

"Where then?" Stitts asked. "What did the poem say?"

"Some weird shit… it was all old English. Something about spears and night and… *welkin*, whatever the fuck that means."

"*Welkin*?" Greg repeated from the backseat, pulling out his phone.

"I guess… I don't know," Chase snapped. "Do I look like an English professor? Do I smoke a pipe and have patches on the elbows of my jacket?"

Her frustration mounting again, fueled by the interrogation as well as the traffic, Chase pulled the car onto the soft shoulder and started to drive.

"*From either end of heaven the welkin burns,*" Greg said from the backseat. "Was that it?"

"Yeah, I think so. Something like that, anyway. Where is it from?"

"Milton's *Paradise Lost*."

"Adam and Eve," Stitts chimed. "Also about inequality, Satan, good and evil. Sounds appropriate."

"*Prick forth the airy knights, and couch their spears, Till thickest legions close; with feats of arms, from either end of heaven the welkin burns.* That it?" Greg asked.

"Yeah, pretty sure. Any idea what it means? How it relates to Mike?" Chase asked.

"I'm no scholar," Greg replied, "but I'm not thinking that it's a cry for peace."

"No shit."

Chase had gone no more than a hundred yards on the shoulder before she came up beside a squad car. His cherries immediately flicked on, and the nose of the car inched out to block her path.

"Fuck," she grumbled. Even before the officer got out of the car, she had her badge at the ready.

"Chase Adams, FBI. What's going on here? What's the holdup?"

The officer, sporting a wide-brimmed tan-color hat, hooked a thumb over his left shoulder. Chase followed the man's gaze and noticed a throng of people, a procession of sorts. They were all banging on drums and chanting something that she couldn't quite make out.

"What is it?"

"It's the Las Vegas Golden Knights—it's their first playoff game tonight," the officer said matter-of-factly. He grinned as he spoke, then, after looking around quickly, he untucked the front of his shirt. The officer raised it several inches, revealing a Golden Knights jersey beneath. "Two p.m. start time."

Chase pressed her lips together.

"Cute. Well, is there any way to let me through? I'm on a case and—"

She stopped abruptly and turned to face Greg in the backseat.

"Did the poem say *night* or *knight*? Starts with a 'k' or an 'n'?"

Greg glanced down at his phone.

"*K*—the medieval kind."

Something inside her mind clicked.

"Jesus fucking Christ," she whispered. "Who owns the Vegas Knights? Is it the same people who own The Emerald?"

Greg grimaced.

"I'm not sure. I think—"

"Not a person, but a group," the officer offered. "The Foley Group. And, yeah, I think that they also own a bunch of casinos on the strip, including The Emerald."

Chase slammed her hands down on the wheel.

"I have to get through," she ordered. "You need to stop the procession and let me through. Someone's going to blow up the goddamn stadium."

The officer's face twisted into a mask of confusion and he looked to Stitts for support. When he wasn't given any, he leaned down and peered into the backseat.

Recognition crossed over his features and his expression hardened.

He knew Greg, Chase realized. He knew Greg, and he cared for him as much as Sgt. Theodore did, which was to say not at all.

"I don't think I can do that," the officer said flatly, tucking his uniform back into his pants. "You're going to have to wait until it ends."

"What? Did you hear what I said? Somebody is going to blow up the arena!"

"Ma'am, I understand that you're—"

And there it was again: *ma'am*. Little more in this world bothered Chase as much as being referred to as 'ma'am.'

There was no reasoning with this officer, she knew. Unbuckling her seatbelt, she turned to Stitts.

"You guys meet me there, I'm going to try to cut him off."

Stitts's eyes bulged.

"Chase, you can't—Chase! *Chase!*"

But Chase was already out of the car and running toward the throng of Golden Knight fans.

Chapter 53

STITTS SWORE AS HE hurried around to the driver's seat.

Within two hours of finding Chase again, she was gone. And, once again, there was nothing he could do about it. He considered going after her, of course, but she had disappeared into the crowd before he got his act together.

"You're seriously not going to let us through?" Stitts demanded.

The officer looked as surly as ever.

"I put a call in to Sgt. Theodore, but until I hear back from him, you're going to have to wait in line like everyone else."

Stitts ground his teeth.

"If anyone dies today, it's on you, you fucking prick," he said under his breath.

The officer looked shocked, but Stitts rolled up his window before he had the chance to reply. Then, when the man took a step back and reached for his walkie again, Stitts swerved around the nose of his vehicle and continued along the soft shoulder.

In the rearview, he saw the officer shouting and waving his arms, but he ignored him. Several other cars honked as he passed, but Stitts paid them no heed. If he was forced to wait for the procession, then he would at least be the first in line.

The problem was, the line of fans seemed *endless*. Even craning his neck, Stitts couldn't find the tail.

"Sure made some friends here in Las Vegas, didn't you, Greg?" he muttered.

Immediately after the words left his mouth, however, Stitts regretted saying them. And when he caught the reflection of the man in the rearview, his eyes downcast, he felt even worse.

"I'm sorry, I'm just frustrated. Ever since..."

... I picked up Chase from Grassroots, things have been difficult, Stitts nearly said. Instead, he went with, "... the case started, it's just been one problem after another."

"Tell me about it."

Stitts huffed.

"Speaking of which, it looks like we're going to be here for a while. Why don't you tell me what happened when you got hit in the leg?"

"I told you already; it happened during the Village shooting."

Stitts looked up at the man in the mirror again.

"You sure did. But why don't you tell me what *really* happened?"

Greg frowned, then he tucked his chin into his chest. At first, Stitts thought that the man would reiterate the lie he'd told before, but when he finally started to speak, there was no doubt that this was the truth. Stitts didn't need Chase's poker skills to figure this one out; it was in his face, his voice, his entire body.

"It was... it was pandemonium," Greg began slowly. "At first, nobody even knew what was happening. We all thought the sounds were part of the concert. It wasn't until the first few people started dropping that we knew that something was terribly wrong. And even then, the concert was so large and loud that I couldn't communicate with the other officers. I was shouting for everyone to get down, to lie on the ground, to stay still, but barely anyone listened. There was... there was just so much blood.

"I was trying to shuttle people through the gates, to get them out of the kill zone, but everyone was pushing and shoving. It was craziness. I needed help to try and control them, but I'd somehow lost my partner in the crowd. Eventually, I found him," Greg hesitated and took a moment to wipe tears from his eyes. "There was this small wall toward the south end of the Village, about shoulder high. My partner was trying to get over it, to climb to safety. For a second, I locked eyes with him and I saw that he was terrified, just completely overwhelmed by fear. He was trying to get over the wall over and over again, but it was slick with blood and he kept slipping.

"Everyone was scared—shit I was petrified—and I didn't really blame him for trying to get out. The problem was, he was so pumped up with adrenaline—fight-or-flight and all that—that he didn't even realize that there was a woman and her small child cowering beneath him. Every time he tried to climb up, he'd fall back down again. He was stepping all over them, kicking them, kneeing them, and he didn't even know it. Instinct took over, and I ran to my partner, yelling at him to stop, to go around, but he wouldn't listen."

Greg was fully crying now and Stitts was surprised that he had tears in his own eyes.

"When I finally got to him, I pulled him off the wall and shoved him away from the woman, who was barely conscious, and her wailing toddler. That's when… that's when… fuck… that's when a bullet hit my partner in the chest. I couldn't do anything for him… I couldn't even get to him even though he almost certainly died instantly. Bullets suddenly hit the pavement all around us, and I did the only thing I could think of: I wrapped my body around the woman and child. That's when I got hit in the leg."

Stitts took a deep breath and collected himself. He couldn't imagine the horror, the helplessness this man and the others at the concert must have felt.

"But why… why won't anyone talk to you? What you did… that was heroic."

Greg averted his gaze.

"One of the other officers saw me, and with the panic, he thought I was just running from the scene. He thought that I pushed my partner out of the way to save myself, and it cost him his life."

Stitts finally understood why everyone at the LVMPD hated Greg so much and why he was confined to the station. Not only did they consider him a coward and untrustworthy, but they thought him a liability as well.

"And why haven't you told anyone this?" Stitts asked.

Greg shrugged.

"I didn't want to dishonor my partner's memory. Despite what he did, he was a good man and a good cop. He just had a baby… and as a father myself, I couldn't imagine growing up with people saying things about him, calling him a coward."

"But even after… after they shunned you?" Stitts asked. He didn't care for the word 'shunned,' but couldn't come up with anything more appropriate in the moment.

"My family understands… they know me, and even though they don't know the whole story, they know that I wouldn't run. But my partner's daughter… she's just a baby. If I told people what really happened, she would grow up thinking that her dad was something he wasn't. It's bad enough that she lost her dad, but to lose her dad and everyone call him a coward? That would be worse. *Much* worse."

Silence fell over the vehicle for several minutes before Greg spoke up again.

"If you want to let Sgt. Theodore know what's going on… tell him that you think there's a bomb at the arena… I think that it would be better coming from you," he said.

Stitts thought back to his last encounter with the sergeant, the man's smug expression and his mock wave.

"Yeah, I'm not so sure about that."

Chapter 54

There was no way that Chase could find Mike Hartman in the procession of thousands of rowdy fans as they walked from the strip toward the arena.

And yet she did.

She spotted the Timex watch first and then recognized the man's shape next. At some point since the first massacre, he had dyed his hair blond and was now wearing an oversized Golden Knights jersey, but she knew it was him.

Chase weaved her way through the crowd, trying to make it to Mike who was roughly fifty or so people ahead of her. Progress was difficult, as everyone was shouting some sort of annoying chant, or banging on drums and wagging foam fingers that kept obscuring her vision.

"Get out of my way!" she shouted. "Get the hell out of my way!"

Chase elbowed several people in the ribs, and when they bent protectively, she slipped by them. Her movements became less subtle as the pace of the crowd picked up until she was simply resorting to pushing or shoving her way through.

"Hey lady, wait your turn!" a man shouted as she passed.

Her aggressive nature paid off; in less than ten minutes, she made it to Mike. Trying not to draw any additional attention to herself, Chase slipped her hand onto the butt of her revolver tucked beneath her jacket. With her other hand, she grabbed the man's shoulder and pulled, only this time she wasn't trying to make it through but spin him around.

As he turned, Chase began to pull the revolver out and then stopped suddenly.

"Go Knights, go!" the man shouted in her face.

Chase stumbled backward. The man had eyes that were close-set, a narrow nose, and a large space between his two front teeth.

It wasn't Mike Hartman. It wasn't even *close* to Mike Hartman.

Chase swore and shoved by the man, trying to make her way to the front of the procession.

As she hurried, her eyes were focused on hands and wrists, trying to pick out the Timex.

Chase knew that Mike was here somewhere; she just knew it.

He *had* to be.

And if he *was* here, and if she touched him... well, it wouldn't be like the bartender back on the seventh floor of The Emerald. She hadn't seen anything then because that man wasn't involved in the shooting. He'd been a corpse that Mike and his crew had stolen from the morgue; he had nothing to tell her. But if she grabbed Mike, she'd *see* the way she'd *seen* when Frank Carruthers had grasped her arm in Chicago.

Chase hadn't lost her touch, she just hadn't touched the right man.

"Get out of the way!" she shouted, all elbows and knees now.

Her goal had changed; it wasn't to find Mike Hartman, something that was close to impossible, she realized, but to get to the arena. Chase imagined that Stitts was trying to convince Sgt. Theodore to postpone the game, to cordon off the arena, but was skeptical of his success.

She was nearly running now, elbowing people as she passed, desperate to get by. In the distance, the arena loomed large, a swooping, sand-colored structure.

One-hundred yards, eighty, sixty.

When Chase was less than forty yards from the entrance, the line simply stopped moving. She tried to shove her way through as she had done for most of the procession, but here the crowd was too thick.

By staying low, her small frame finally an asset, Chase managed to weave to the outside of the line and glanced toward the arena. The front of the line seemed to be logjammed at the security checkpoint.

Chase had no idea how Mike was planning on getting the bomb into the arena, but based on her experience with Sgt. Theodore, she was putting no faith in the arena rent-a-cops.

"Let me through! FBI!"

Her words were soaked up by the ubiquitous *Go Knights, Go* chant.

Frustrated, Chase leaned out once more and something caught her eye.

Everyone seemed to be either stopped or in the process of making their way through the security gates except for one person. And while he was too far away to see if he was wearing a watch, the man was sporting a Knights jersey that was bulky—awkwardly so. His middle was much thicker than the spindly legs coming out of his khaki shorts.

Chase couldn't be certain that it was him, but she was at her wit's end. In one day, she'd seen people she played cards with over the course of several hours mowed down in a hail of bullets. She had once again treated Stitts like a piece of shit, and she'd cried with a woman who'd lost her husband, which had led her son to murder. The last thing she wanted was for anybody else to die today.

An image of the pills that she had swallowed back it Grassroots flashed in her mind then, as did the face of the woman who had saved her. Louisa, who claimed that they had something in common, and the same woman that Chase had punched in the face and broken her nose, had saved her life. The woman owed her nothing, and yet she hadn't hesitated when it came to saving Chase.

And Chase was beginning to think that it was for a reason. She wasn't big on faith, karma, grace, a calling, or anything like that, but the fact was, she was alive because of Louisa. If she failed now, if anybody else died, that would be on her. Because if she had taken her own life back at Grassroots, then maybe Stitts would have teamed up with a different agent, a better one, one who wasn't as fucked-up as she, one who could have stopped this craziness before it got really bad.

Without realizing it, Chase's hand found its way back into her coat again. This time when she felt the butt of her gun, she didn't hesitate.

She pulled it out and pointed it to the sky.

"Everybody down!" Chase shouted at the top of her lungs. "Everybody, *get down!*"

Then she squeezed off a round.

Chapter 55

WHEN AT LONG LAST there was a break in the procession of people, it transitioned into a procession of cars. Even though Stitts had bullied his way to the front, there was still a glut of vehicles trying to make it into the parking lot. Unsure of what to do next, he looked to Greg in the backseat.

"This is nuts," he said. "Someone's about to blow up the arena, and we're stuck in traffic. Do you think you can—"

Stitts stopped mid-sentence. His gaze had drifted back to the crowd of people and he found himself staring at a petite woman off to one side who was facing the arena.

"Chase? What the hell? What—no! *No!*"

As he watched, Chase pulled out her service pistol and aimed upward.

"What are you—"

The drumroll was punctuated by the sound of a gun report. Even though it was only marginally louder than the sound of the crowd—the drums, the chants, the shrill shrieks of expectant joy—people seem to be attuned to it, what with the Village shooting a not too distant memory.

And pandemonium ensued.

Roughly a third of the people closest to Chase immediately dropped to the ground and covered their heads with their hands, while the rest scattered. Most of them ran back toward the strip, correctly assuming that it would be safer there.

In the distance, the police officers and security near the arena entrance started barking orders, but with people running in every direction, it was impossible for them to determine exactly where the shot had come from.

But Stitts knew. He knew because his eyes were locked on Chase as she ran toward the arena.

She was on a collision course with men who were amped up and had weapons drawn, something that he knew from experience wouldn't end well.

Stitts had no choice but to get out of the car, draw his own weapon, and run after her.

Chapter 56

CHASE TUCKED HER GUN out of sight—not back in the holster, but pressed it against her thigh—just in case some testosterone-ridden officer tried to take her out.

Despite the chaos around her, she somehow managed to keep her eyes locked on the man who was getting through—no, not *through*, but around the metal detectors and without being searched.

Her plan had backfired; in the confusion, it only made it easier for the man who she was now convinced was Mike Hartman to slip inside the arena.

"Shit," she swore as she sprinted toward the doors.

As one of the few people moving toward, and not away, from the arena, it wasn't long before Chase drew the ire of police and security alike.

Several men stepped forward, their pistols drawn.

"Drop the gun!" someone shouted.

Shit.

She hadn't thought this through. Not at all.

Chase had no choice but to comply and was in the process of raising her arms and shouting that she was FBI when something struck her side and she went down.

Hard.

Chase cried out but didn't struggle; she knew that if she struggled, it would only make things worse. Hot breath was suddenly on her ear, and a man was whispering something about how she was going to jail for a long time or something equally as annoying and clichéd.

"I'm FBI," she grumbled. The officer's response was to put further pressure on her back and arms. She could feel the man struggling to get the handcuffs on her, but he was so hopped up on testosterone that he was having a hard go of it.

"I'm FBI, for Christ's sake," Chase shouted. "Check my coat! My badge is in my coat!"

Once again, her words went unheeded.

Just as the first cuff was slapped on her wrist, she heard someone else shout similar words to the ones she struggled to get out.

"FBI! Let her go!"

In response to the shout, the officer on Chase's back leaned away from her a little, which gave her just enough room to turn her head. To her surprise, Chase saw Stitts coming toward her with something in his hand. But unlike her, it wasn't a gun; it was his badge.

"FBI, let her go."

A different officer took the reins now.

"Stay back. Just stay back."

"All I have is a badge," Stitts continued, holding it higher for all to see. "I'm an FBI agent and so is she. Please, just let her up."

As when Chase had made the claim, no one seemed to give a shit.

"Just stay back," several officers said in unison.

Chase felt the man on her back apply additional pressure and hook her other wrist in the cuffs. Before she realized what was happening, Chase was hoisted to her feet.

"I told you I was FBI, let me go—I need to get inside. A bomb is going to go off."

Although the officer didn't reply, his grip on her arms, raised up the small of her back, relaxed a little.

"All I have is a badge—my gun is tucked in the holster. My name is Jeremy Stitts and the woman you just slapped cuffs on is FBI Special Agent Chase Adams. Call your boss—call Sgt. Theodore, he'll tell you."

The officer said something that Chase didn't pick up, and Stitts reiterated his statement.

She was beginning to regret her decision to draw her gun in a crowd. What in god's name made her think that that was a good idea?

"Thomas, it's me," a new voice shouted, one that Chase also recognized. "It's Greg Ivory. They're serious; they're FBI Agents, and there's a bomb inside the arena."

Chapter 57

"I'm not fucking around, Thomas. You *know* me."

There was an uncomfortable pause, one that Stitts feared would end with him eating a bullet or having his wrists cuffed. But cooler heads prevailed and, before he really knew what was happening, someone grabbed his badge from his hand and inspected it as if it were the original copy of the Declaration of Independence.

The man shrugged.

"Looks good to me," he said over his shoulder. And with those two words, the temperature of the situation suddenly changed.

The suspicion was off Stitts, and he was able to move freely without fear of being shot. He went directly to the man with the most severe expression on his face, assuming that he was in charge.

"You need to let her go," Stitts said sternly.

The man, who Stitts had correctly pegged as the one in charge, shook his head.

"I'm keeping her until Sgt. Theodore says so—she fired her pistol into a goddamn crowd."

Stitts scowled.

"It was a warning shot. There's a—"

A hand came down on his shoulder, and Stitts whipped around. He relaxed when he saw it was Greg, who gave him a nod.

"Tom, you know me," he said. "You know that—"

"I know that you got your partner killed," the man whom Greg had called Tom spat. "That's what I know."

Greg hobbled forward on his cane.

"You also know that I don't play games, Tom. This is no joke. People are in danger."

There was a short impasse, which was eventually broken by Tom who lowered his gaze and walked over to the man who held Chase by the wrists.

"Let her go," he instructed.

When the man started to protest, Tom clenched his jaw.

"Let her go," he repeated, and this time the man obliged and uncuffed Chase.

Stitts expected Chase to come to him, or at the very least to glare at the man who had knocked her roughly to the ground, but she did neither.

Chase's singular focus was on the arena entrance.

As Tom got on his phone to check with Sgt. Theodore, Stitts saw Chase bend, pick up her pistol, and then slowly sidle toward the arena. Stitts reflexively started after her, but Tom held up a hand, halting his forward progress.

Several seconds later, Tom turned back to Stitts.

"I'm sorry for the misunderstanding, Agent Stitts, and you too, Chase. But Sgt. Theodore said there's no way that we're going to shut down the very first playoff game in Las Vegas Golden Knight history. If you need to go inside and check the place out, go right ahead. We've got canines on the way, and the bomb squad on call, but without solid intel, the puck will drop at two p.m."

"Solid intel?" Stitts spat back. "I've just told you—"

Greg squeezed his shoulder, effectively silencing him, and Stitts took a deep breath. Even though Sgt. Theodore was wavering on his claim that he wouldn't offer them assistance, Stitts was worried that it wasn't enough.

If Chase was right, not only should they close down the arena, but perhaps the entire Las Vegas strip as well.

Chapter 58

"**THAT MAN, THE ONE** that just entered, why didn't you search him?" Chase accused, pointing a finger at the security guard who stood with his hands jammed into the pockets of his k-way coat.

The man looked like a deer in the headlights, his large eyes charcoal briquettes embedded in unleavened dough.

"That guy? He was here yesterday. Brought in oil for the fryers."

Yesterday? Shit...

"Why didn't you search him?"

The man's eyes flicked to the person to his right, and then the police officer to his left. And Chase immediately knew why: Mike Hartman had slipped him some cash that he wouldn't be searched.

"God damn it," Chase muttered.

Yesterday... he was here yesterday, planning this. Last night's attack on the poker game was just a last-minute fuck you to the players.

"Forget it," she snapped. "The oil... where did he go with the oil?"

"I dunno, I didn't follow him or nothin'. Lady, I didn't know nothin' about this. He had ID and everything. Said he was just a cook, working the fryers upstairs."

Chase bit her lip in frustration.

"Where did he go?" she yelled. "Where the fuck do the cooks go?"

"I dunno—"

"*For fuck's sake!*"

"Yesterday, I let him and his truck into the garage."

Truck? He had an entire truck?

Chase's heart was racing now. Even though the majority of the procession had scattered, there were likely already people inside... hundreds of them.

"Where's the garage?" Chase demanded. "Is it on this side?"

The security guard shook his head.

"No, it's all the way on the other side of the arena. But the best way to get there by foot is to go through here and then take the stairs on the left."

The man hadn't even finished his sentence before Chase was off again, passing through the metal detector that chimed like the Hell's Bells as she ran by.

The inside of T-Mobile arena was more packed than she had expected. It appeared as if a good portion of the procession had already made it inside.

As soon as she stepped into the stadium, Chase realized that she'd been wrong: there weren't hundreds of fans inside, but *thousands* of them. They were everywhere, milling about, drinking beer, scarfing hot dogs, and shoveling palmfuls of popcorn into their mouths.

They were oblivious to the danger that they were in.

With renewed vigor, Chase twisted her way between the fans and made her way toward the stairwell tucked behind a concession stand. She was hopeful that Sgt. Theodore was on his way, that he was taking so long because he was busy enacting some sort of evacuation plan, but deep down, Chase doubted it. The asshole was probably staring in a mirror somewhere, repeating "Lieutenant Theodore" over and over again.

Shaking her head in frustration, Chase slammed her hands against the door, which was marked with EMERGENCY ONLY.

Well, she thought, *if this isn't an emergency, I don't know what is.*

A small bell chimed from somewhere above her head, an annoying pinging sound that Chase supposed constituted an alarm. Normally, she wouldn't have wanted the attention called to her, but in this situation, Chase wished the alarm was ten times as loud—an air raid siren, perhaps. Anything to get the place to clear out.

Chase took the stairs two at a time, heading past the first door marked EMPLOYEES ONLY, before arriving at a second with GARAGE across the top.

When she spotted the key card scanner next to the door handle, her heart sunk. Chase hadn't thought to ask the security guard for access to the lower levels—she'd been so eager to hurry after the man who she thought was Mike Hartman, that it hadn't occurred to her. And now it looked like she was going to have to go back up and waste more time that she didn't have.

But as Chase neared the door, she realized that someone had propped it open by jamming a wedge of wood in the top. She silently slipped through, making sure to replace the piece of wood in case she had to make a quick exit.

It was a garage all right, she didn't need to see the concrete pillars or the markings on the ground to know that much.

The acrid smell of oil and gasoline caused her nose to scrunch.

To her right, Chase noted several large vans, one of which was covered in a Golden Knights wrap. To her left was a catering van and several wheelchair-accessible vehicles.

Chase moved quietly now, knowing that stealth was an important factor in whether or not she made it out of the garage alive. She didn't have to work too hard, however, given the crowd's sounds from above. Withdrawing her pistol, she sidled up next to the Las Vegas Golden Knights team bus and moved along its length.

When Chase got to the end, she poked her head out, then retracted it immediately. She repeated this several times, then stitched together the individual visuals to form a cohesive image.

Near the center of the garage, not parked in a spot but wedged between two huge concrete pillars, was a truck that looked as if it had come straight from a construction site. It was a faded red, with patches of rust filling nearly every seam. A dark blue tarp had been laid over the truck bed, but it was clear by the way it bulged that it wasn't empty.

Caterer my ass.

Chase stepped out into the open, then crept slowly around the rear of the truck, scanning the interior as she went. With a deep breath, she swung around the other side, and that's when she saw him.

He was on one knee, his back to her, but Chase knew that it was the same man that she'd seen outside in the bulky Knights jersey. His hands were out of sight, but the way his shoulders moved, it was clear that he was fidgeting with something.

With another deep breath, Chase raised her gun.

"Mike Hartman? I need you to stop what you're doing and put your hands in the air."

Chapter 59

THE MAN IN THE Golden Knights jersey slowly rose to his feet, but he only lifted his right hand in the air. Even then, the angle of the arm was wrong, and it took Chase a few moments to realize that this was the shoulder that had been shot. She thought the material on that side of the jersey was darker too, as if soaked with blood.

"Both hands," Chase shouted. "Put *both* hands in the air, right now!"

"I don't think you want me to do that," the man replied calmly.

As he spoke, he slowly started to turn and Chase made sure to level her pistol at center mass. She also prepared herself to dive behind the Golden Knights team bus should he be aiming a weapon at her.

The first thing Chase noticed was that it was indeed Mike Hartman, the second was that he was grinning. She even saw the cheap Timex watch on his left wrist, as if she needed further corroboration.

"I said, put—"

Chase's eyes fell on his left hand and she gasped.

Mike was clutching something that looked like a thick pen between his fingers, one that had wires extending from the base and disappearing beneath the hem of his jersey.

No, Chase most definitely didn't want him to raise his hand above his head and let go of the deadman's switch. If he did, whatever explosives Mike had beneath that jersey would turn them both into ragu.

"Neat, isn't it?" Mike said, turning the switch in his hand. "Got the materials from work, but the plans? Downloaded them. You'd be surprised what you can find online... well, maybe not. You look young enough to know how to use the internet, maybe even computers. Not like your Luddite of a boss, Sgt. Theodore. Couldn't even track down a goddamn complaint."

Chase squinted as she took this in.

"He's not my boss. But you're right; he's an asshole."

Mike took a step forward, and Chase extended the gun.

"Okay, okay," he said. "Wait… you were there! You were at the poker game. How the—how…" he chuckled and shook his head. "Who knew cops could play poker?"

"I'm not a cop. I'm FBI," Chase said, stalling. She needed Sgt. Theodore or Stitts to arrive soon and help her either talk this guy down or figure out a way to disarm him.

She was leaning toward the latter.

"Cop, FBI, what does it matter? You're all useless. Twenty-seven years my dad worked for the casino, and when he died because of the smoke and the stress, you know what he got? Nothing. Not a red cent."

"The rich get richer," Chase said absently.

The comment took Mike by surprise and he fell silent. Chase used the confusion to her advantage and, with her free hand, lifted the corner of the tarp on the back of the truck.

In the truck bed were several large barrels marked in large letters with 'RDX' and EXPLOSIVE.

"Just something to celebrate the very first playoff game," Mike said, regaining his composure. "Help the Knights come out with a bang. Oh, I know what you're thinking. How is it possible that I could come down here with just a shitty fake ID claiming to be a caterer and park a truck loaded with over a hundred pounds of RDX? How's that possible? Well, I'll tell you how that's possible, lady."

"Chase."

"Excuse me?"

"My name's not *lady*—it's Chase."

The man observed her curiously before continuing.

"Okay, Chase, sure; you want to know how I did it?"

Come on, Stitts, where are you?

"I know how you did it. In fact, I know how you did everything. I know that you faked your own death with a corpse and a tattoo, I know that you put up false windows after you escaped the room to confuse us, I also know that your buddy Peter came back to put the real ones up the next day. I know that you set off those bombs just to draw attention away from yourself and the real plan. So... how'd you get in here? I bet you just greased a few palms," Chase shrugged. "That's all it takes."

Mike Hartman blinked several times, his face going slack before the grin reappeared.

"Not bad, not bad. Not a revelation, mind you; that's just how things work. If you have money, you can pretty much do whatever the fuck you want. You can screw over an old, retiring man who spent the better portion of his life working for you, and not give him a goddamn cent in severance. Even the insurance company managed to weasel out of their contract. Why? Because he had weed in his system? It was secondhand from one of the private games that he was dealing at to make some extra cash. Even the police—the ones who are supposed to protect *us*, normal, regular citizens—don't give a shit. Probably got a handout from the casino and insurance company *not to* look for the complaint that my father filed."

Chase was content to just let Mike talk, but when his face started to turn red, she decided that it would be in both of their best interests to defuse the situation.

"Paradise is lost, isn't that right, Mike?"

For the third time since entering the garage, he was taken aback.

"How do you—"

"But let me ask you something," Chase interrupted. "Who's the good guy here? You? Me? You've got the cash now and you can do whatever you want. You can just get the hell out of here and drive to anywhere in the country. Start over. You don't have to do this. You don't have to kill all these innocent people."

The man balked.

"Innocent? Innocent… really? Nobody here is innocent. These people… they're all contributing to the rich getting richer. They couldn't even give my father a couple hundred bucks to help my mother with the cost of the funeral, but they can buy a hockey team for half a billion dollars? Every single person in this arena, every person who supports this team, lines their pockets."

Chase found her own frustration mounting.

"So, what? You get to be a martyr? You think that anything you do here is going to matter? You blow up this fucking place, kill all these people, and you know what they'll do? They'll rebuild. They'll make it bigger, they'll make it more expensive, and they'll blame it all on you, Mike. How do you think that will make your mother feel?"

"My mother? My *mother*? You leave her out of this."

"Leave her out of it? You really think that's going to happen? The media will be all over her, hounding her, asking about you, whether you were spanked or had your pecker touched as a child."

Mike sneered.

"I gave her enough money to get out of here."

"What? The half a mill? That'll be gone in six months, a year, tops. Trust me, I've seen it before. Then she'll be back here, in the very place that you condemned, asking the very people you scorned for a handout. Trust me, Mike."

The man's expression softened, and Chase thought that she was getting somewhere. But then he broke into a grin, and her hopes were dashed.

"Trust you? *Trust you?* I can't trust you. I can't trust anyone. How does the old saying go? The only things that are certain in life are death and taxes. But these large companies, they don't even pay taxes, do they? Hiding money in offshore accounts, getting breaks so long as they fund certain election campaigns." Mike held out the deadman's trigger. "But I'm guessing that for all their power, wealth, and influence, they can't get out of death. What do you think?"

Movement behind Mike suddenly caught Chase's eye.

Finally, Stitts! It's about fucking time!

Chapter 60

But it wasn't Stitts; the figure was shorter and slightly stooped. Her initial instinct was that it was Peter Doherty or Tony Ballucci coming to lend Mike a hand.

Except this was Mike's calling, not theirs; they'd only been in it for the money.

"I think you're off your fucking rocker, that's what I think. You think suicide will change anything? You think that it ever changes *anything*?"

Mike's face contorted then, twisting into a mix of emotions that ranged from anger to frustration and ultimately, to sadness. But then that stupid grin returned.

"Oh, you're good," he said with a hint of joviality. "In fact, I'd say that you sound like someone who has considered the act yourself, isn't that right?"

It was Chase's turn to protest.

"I wouldn't—"

As if they were in a high school classroom and you needed the talking stick to speak, Mike held the deadman's trigger out to her.

"No, nothing as dramatic as this. But maybe… maybe you thought about taking a couple extra sleeping pills one night, or just letting the wheel go when you're on an empty road. Oh, you've contemplated doing something like this—I can see it in your eyes. You stand there all high and mighty with your gun and your badge… you think you've never hurt people?"

Chase took a deep, shuddering breath as her mind turned to the fateful day when Georgina had been taken from her.

"Oh, I've hurt people," Chase said softly. And it was the truth; she'd hurt Georgina, she'd hurt Brad and Felix, and she'd hurt Jeremy Stitts. She'd hurt a lot of people during her thirty-five years and would undoubtedly hurt more before her time was up. But she wasn't perfect, and never claimed to be. Words that Dr. Matteo used during one of their first encounters suddenly occurred to her.

Live in the moment, Chase. We can't go back and change what we did in the past, and we can't with any degree of certainty predict what will happen in the future. All we can do is control our actions right here, right now, in this moment.

"But there's a difference between you and me," she continued.

Mike raised an eyebrow.

"And what's that?"

The crowd above suddenly worked itself into a frenzy, and Chase could hear them chanting, *Go Knights, Go!* It was so loud that Mike Hartman's eyes drifted upward.

"I didn't go through with it," Chase muttered.

And that's when the shadowy figure chose to strike.

He leaped onto Mike Hartman's back, wrapping his arms around the man's chest.

"Grab his hand!" Chase shouted. "Don't let him let go of the trigger!"

She sprinted towards the duo as she yelled, tucking the gun in her holster at the same time.

Mike bucked and spun around, but he was unable to dislodge the man on his back. Chase shouted again for him to grab Mike's left hand, but she was just wasting words; he had already wrapped his hand overtop of Mike's, making it impossible for him to pull his thumb away from the deadman's trigger.

Chase was within several feet of them now, and she realized that their savior wasn't Stitts or even Knights security. Greg Ivory; the man with the limp who had helped them ever since they'd arrived in Las Vegas, was draped over Mike Hartman like an organic backpack.

"Get off me," Mike Hartman shouted from between clenched teeth. "Get the fuck off me!"

Chase delivered a kick to the front of Mike's left knee. He cried out as his leg buckled and he went down. With one of Greg's arms wrapped around his chest and the other holding his hand, Mike was unable to brace himself. His nose and chin cracked audibly off the concrete floor and blood immediately erupted from both wounds.

"Hold his hand," Chase repeated. "Hold it tight!"

As Mike's eyes rolled back in his head, Chase got on one knee and lifted the man's jersey.

What she saw took her breath away.

Attached to Mike's chest was a myriad of wires connecting to what looked like a homemade science kit. The box attached to his sternum was clear, and inside there were two liquids: one white and one tinted yellow, separated by a plastic partition.

Chase knew little about explosives outside of her FBI general training, but she knew better than to start messing around with something that looked like a prop from Short Circuit. Based on their proximity to the pickup truck, if she made a mistake and those two liquids mixed, it wouldn't just be the three of them going up, but most of the arena as well.

"Fuck," she muttered.

Mike moaned and his eyelids fluttered.

"My leg," Greg said, his own face twisted in anguish. "My leg... I can't... I can't get up."

Heart racing, Chase took a step back and observed the scene, trying to figure what to do next. Mike was on the ground with Greg on top of him, their left hands wrapped together as if in prayer.

"Are you sure? You can't pull him up?" But even as Chase asked the question, she knew the answer.

"I don't think so," Greg replied.

Chase pulled her cell phone out of her pocket but had zero reception beneath the arena.

She swore again.

"Where's Stitts? The bomb squad? Please tell me they're on their way."

Greg might've gotten the jump on Mike, taken him by surprise, but he was younger and stronger than the aged police officer. When he came to, Chase wasn't sure how long Greg would be able to stay on top of him.

"Stitts was outside... talking to the police... I snuck around—" he groaned and Chase saw his leg seize. "—I don't know how long it'll take for them to get down here."

Chase ground her teeth and her eyes flicked from the two men on the ground to the truck just a few feet from them.

Her first priority was to make sure that the arena didn't blow up. When that was taken care of, she would deal with making sure that they all made it out of this alive.

"Can you roll?" Chase asked.

Greg nodded.

"I think so," he said, but the grunt of pain that followed made Chase question his confidence.

But she couldn't think of anything else at that moment.

"You have to roll away from the truck. Roll away from the truck, and then we're going to switch places."

Greg's eyes widened.

"Switch places?" he shook his head. "No way. *No way*. Go get help, Chase. I can hold him. Trust me."

Chase, torn now, looked back the way she'd come. And then she started to yell.

"Help! Somebody help us! Call the police! Help! *Help!*"

Greg continued to shake his head.

"It's no use. They can't hear you over the crowd. Just go, Chase. I'll roll away from the truck."

Chase's eyes whipped back and forth from Greg, to the truck, to the stairwell door behind them.

"Fuck!" she screamed.

Mike moaned loudly then and Chase made up her mind.

"Just, please, hold him tight, Greg. I'll be back in just a minute, okay?"

Chase was about to turn towards the door when Greg's cool blue eyes leveled at her.

"Tell my wife and daughter I love them, and that I'm sorry," he said quietly. "That I'm not a coward."

Chase shook her head.

"You can tell them yourself."

With that, Chase turned and ran. She sprinted past the team bus, then the line of wheelchair vans. Behind her, she heard several grunts and a sound that she presumed was Greg rolling with Mike.

She didn't look back, didn't glance over her shoulder; she just ran.

Chase had just thrown the door wide when she heard another sound: an audible pop, followed by a fizz as if someone had just opened a bottle of champagne.

Only this was no celebration.

Chase ducked and then the bomb went off.

Chapter 61

STITTS WAS ON THE second to last step when he felt the pressure in the stairwell change.

"Chase!" he screamed.

He leaped to the landing just as his partner's body was launched into him. She struck his chest, sending them both to the ground and knocking the wind out of him.

Stitts grunted and wrapped his arms protectively around her, squeezing her tight.

Before the door rebounded, Stitts saw a flash of yellow and orange in the garage. All four tires of a Golden Knights bus lifted off the ground, only to come crashing back down with a metallic groan a second later.

Then the door banged closed and Stitts turned his gaze to the woman in his arms.

"You're okay," he said, his voice hitching. "You did it, Chase. You saved everyone."

Her eyes filled with tears.

"I didn't," she croaked. "Greg… Greg did."

Chapter 62

"TODAY, IT IS WITH great sadness that I stand before you as lieutenant and share the terrible news that Las Vegas has lost one of its own. Earlier this evening, Officer Gregory Ivory, a veteran of thirty plus years on the force, lost his life while on duty. While the details of exactly what happened are still unfolding, what we do know is that Greg died a hero, someone who sacrificed himself to keep the residents and forth-three million annual visitors to Las Vegas safe."

Chase wiped a tear that spilled down her cheek and watched as a solemn-looking Lt. Theodore continued to speak.

"I've known Greg personally for more than a dozen years and I'm honored to call him my friend. It is with this in mind that I am proud to announce the Ivory Legacy Fund, an initiative of Greg's daughter, Wynonna, his wife Bethany, and all of the LVMPD. The Ivory Legacy Fund will offer support to officers in Las Vegas who perform otherworldly acts of bravery to keep us all safe."

Chase's eyes drifted from Lt. Theodore to the aforementioned Ivory family. Greg's thirteen-year-old daughter was sobbing into her mother's sweater, while the latter struggled to keep her own emotions in check.

As the ceremony wound down and Lt. Theodore said his final words, Chase was amazed that the man managed to completely avoid mentioning anything about the bomb.

About how Greg managed to roll far enough away from the pickup truck so that the RDX didn't explode. That he had had the foresight to shelter the blast by rolling beneath the Golden Knights' team bus.

No one would ever know what happened under that bus, which suited Chase just fine: she didn't care if Greg was overpowered or if he had just proactively set off the bomb.

None of that mattered; what mattered was that he'd sacrificed himself to save *them*.

Stitts suddenly appeared at her side, his face red. He thrust a black bag into her arms.

"Is that it?" she asked out of the corner of her mouth.

Stitts nodded.

"It was nearly impossible to get it out of evidence, but the newly minted lieutenant decided that he'd look the other way so long as we 'forgot' his indiscretions."

"Figures," Chase said as she took the bag. "Prick forth the airy knights and couch their spears."

"What's that?"

Chase shook her head.

"Nothing. Can you wait here a moment? There are a couple of loose ends I need to tie up before we head back to Quantico."

Stitts didn't argue; Chase got the impression that he was through arguing with her for a long while.

"Go on, then. Our flight's in four hours. Try not to be late."

Chase turned her attention back to the podium. She waited until Wynonna and Bethany Ivory made their way off the stage with a police escort before approaching.

The nearest officer recognized her and gave her a nod as she neared.

"I'll only be a minute," Chase told him as she laid a gentle hand on Bethany's shoulder. The woman stared at Chase with tears in her eyes.

"Were you a friend of Greg's?" she asked quietly.

Chase nodded.

"I was. And I just want to say that your husband was a great man," she said. "And I also wanted to make a donation to your new fund, or feel free to use it for whatever you want."

Chase held the bag out as she spoke, but Bethany only looked at it, a confused expression on her sad face.

"Please," Chase pleaded. "It's what Greg would've wanted."

The woman reluctantly took the bag. When she finally got around to looking inside, her eyes widened.

"But—but—this is too much."

"I'm very sorry for your loss," Chase said, ignoring the woman's comment. "Greg was a hero, now *and* before. Don't let anybody tell you differently."

Chapter 63

STITTS WATCHED CHASE HAND over the bag to Mrs. Ivory before walking toward the podium.

He had no idea where Chase was headed next and didn't bother asking. While he cared for her very much, Stitts had come to realize that she was an enigma and trying to understand what went on in her head was something that would only serve to infuriate him.

After shaking Lt. Theodore's hand, he thanked the man for his hospitality in Las Vegas. It was bullshit, of course; applesauce niceties that were necessary for the next time the FBI needed to work with the ATF, DoD, or local PD.

It was Vegas, after all; there most definitely would be a next time.

The stern-faced man nodded and shook his hand but refrained from a reciprocal thank you.

That was okay by Stitts. He didn't need thanks. His thanks was knowing that the work that he and Chase—mostly Chase—had put in over the past forthy-eight or so hours had prevented eighteen thousand Las Vegas Golden Knights fans from being blown to smithereens.

With a few hours to kill before the flight, Stitts knew what he had to do. After seeing the sunken faces of the people Greg had left behind, what really mattered was suddenly brought into crystalline focus.

He pulled his cell phone out of his pocket and dialed with a trembling finger.

Even before the call was answered, tears started to stream down Stitts's cheeks and he started to shake uncontrollably.

"Mom? I'm coming home. I miss you and I love you."

Chapter 64

"WELL, YOU LOOK LIKE shit," Stu said with a half-smile. "Again."

Chase shrugged and stepped inside the mansion.

"The man who killed Kevin is dead," she said softly.

The smile slid off Stu's face.

"This is related to what happened at the Golden Knights game, isn't it? The cop that they're heralding as a hero?"

Chase nodded.

"He was."

"I'm sorry that a good man had to die, but I'm glad that the person who murdered Kevin is gone," Stu said. "I knew that you could be counted on to pull through."

Chase hesitated before speaking next.

"I'm not a hooker, you know."

The words surprised Stu, and on some level, Chase as well, even though she had uttered them.

"Excuse me?"

"It's just that I've had some... issues in the past, Stu. And sometimes I just don't know how to deal with my feelings. Instead of tackling my problems dead-on, sometimes I just lash out, do things with my body that—"

"Wait a second," Stu interrupted. "You think... you think that you and I..." He let his sentence trail off and chuckled.

Now it was Chase's turn to raise an eyebrow.

She was almost positive that the two of them had gotten drunk off expensive whiskey and then had sex. She wasn't proud of it, but she'd convinced herself after the fact that what she'd done was necessary for the poker game buy-in.

"You mean we didn't? We didn't have sex?"

Stu laughed again.

"Is that what you thought, Chase? That I gave you the money because we had sex? No, dear, you're not my type. Believe me."

Chase was floored by the revelation.

"But... but we drank and... and I woke up in bed with you."

"Yeah—shit, yeah, you drank alright. But after the whiskey, you just asked me to hold you. Then you started to cry and tell me about Georgina. No monkey business, I swear."

Chase gawked. She couldn't believe it. She hadn't told the full story about what happened that day to anyone for more than two decades. And now, for some bizarre reason, she'd opened up to a man she barely knew?

Chase swallowed hard and nodded. The irony was that she didn't know whether to be relieved or ashamed.

"Well, thank you. I guess."

"No, Chase, thank you. I have a feeling that even though Lt. Theodore will take the credit for what happened yesterday, you were responsible for saving many lives. The FBI should be very grateful that they have you."

Chase scoffed.

"*If* they'll have me back," she said.

"Oh, I wouldn't worry about that," Stu said with a grin.

TRGR, Chase thought absently. *Mike was right about one thing: you have money in this world, you make the rules.*

"We'll see about that," Chase said as she made her way toward the door.

"One last thing, Chase."

Chase turned.

"Yes?"

"How did you do, anyway?"

Chase thought back to the poker game, to before the insanity had begun inside the fourteenth-floor hotel room.

The pot had been nearly a half-million dollars, and she knew that she would've gotten Mishenko to push his stack in, especially with a Q - 6 - Q flop.

She closed her eyes and pictured her hole cards: QQ.

"I did all right," Chase said, looking at Stu again. "And I guess that means you did, too."

"I'm sure you did just fine," Stu said softly.

In her mind, she saw Greg walking toward them, leaning on his cane, telling both her and Stitts that they could stay in his office if the douchebags at the ATF and DoD had confiscated theirs. Then she was reminded of the look of shock on Bethany Ivory's face when she stared into the bag Chase had handed her.

"Don't worry, your donation was greatly appreciated," Chase said as she left the mansion for the final time.

Epilogue

"If I'm back, then I'm back," Chase said, her lip curled in disgust. When neither Director Hampton nor Stitts replied, she continued. "And *this* is the case I want."

She tossed the file folder on the desk and several photographs spilled out, one of which almost landed on Director Hampton's lap.

"This is the case I want," she repeated, her tone softening.

Chase's eyes flicked to the photographs of the young girls' faces and was taken aback by their expressions. Even though these were snapped sometimes months before the girls were kidnapped, they always seemed so shocked and scared in them.

"These girls went missing years ago, but I think there's a link to more recent disappearances. And this is the case I want."

Director Hampton frowned.

"That's not the way it works, Chase. You don't get to pick your cases, we assign them to you. And if it weren't for Stitts here, then—"

"Yeah, I get it: Stitts put his neck on the line for me, but I put more than my neck in danger for eighteen thousand people back in Las Vegas. I don't want to make this a regular thing, and I don't want any special treatment going forward. But this is the case I want, this is the case I *need*."

The Director paused for a moment, then looked over at Stitts. Clearly, Hampton was not used to being the one on the hot seat; he was the one used to calling people out and making decisions.

"She's right," Stitts said, and Chase couldn't help but smile. "I think that these new disappearances *are* related."

No matter how many times Chase lied to him or treated him like shit, Stitts was there for her. He cared for her, that much was clear.

He cared too much.

To Chase's surprise, Director Hampton shrugged and then tossed the file folder back at her, which she somehow managed to catch awkwardly.

"In addition to enemies, it appears as if you also made a friend in Vegas," he grumbled. "A very wealthy friend. So, what the hell, maybe you need some downtime after Las Vegas and a cold case is the perfect solution to both our problems. Any idea where you're going to start?"

Chase was so surprised by the sudden decision that it took her a few moments to collect her thoughts.

She could start back in her hometown, where Georgina was taken, or she could go to Nashville where the last girl was kidnapped from. But something in the back of her mind told her that she might be better off snooping around here, right in Virginia.

Chase's mind flicked to Louisa moments before her fist collided with the woman's nose.

We have something in common, Chase. Maybe we can help each other.

"Yeah," Chase said as she turned toward the door. "I know exactly where I'm going to start."

"Before you leave, there's just one more thing," Director Hampton said. "They found Tony Ballucci, the waiter, in his Vegas apartment. He hung himself right next to the untouched money he'd stolen. And the window washer, Peter Doherty? He was just picked up in Atlantic City. Went apeshit after losing more than a hundred grand in a single blackjack session."

Chase shrugged.

"Can't say I feel bad for them."

"Yeah, but here's the thing: we managed to piece together how much money was on the table that night, approximately, anyway, and it looks like about a half-million dollars is still missing. Any idea where it might be?"

"Nope," Chase replied and left the office. "No idea at all."

They were halfway down the hall when Stitts addressed her.

"You know, you never did tell me what you said to Ms. Hartman after she showed you the bag Mike left her."

Chase sighed and rubbed her temples. She had another headache coming on.

"I told her to take the money and get the hell out of Vegas. Start a new life somewhere, forget about the past."

Stitts reached for her arm then, and she turned to face him. For the briefest of moments, Chase thought he was going to kiss her.

What surprised her even more is that she actually leaned into it.

Then he pulled away.

"You really think someone can do that? Move on from such a horrible tragedy?"

Chase shrugged.

"I don't know. Maybe." She chewed the inside of her lip and started walking again. "Probably not."

END

Author's note

I hope you enjoyed this installment of the Chase Adams saga. Next up, *AMBER ALERT*, which is available now. As you probably guessed by the title, in *AMBER ALERT* Chase will come ever closer to finding her sister and dealing with the deep-seated anger and hatred she harbors for herself.

But will she finally find out what happened to Georgina all those years ago? Is it possible that's still alive out there… somewhere?

<u>SPOLER ALERT</u>

Just kidding; who knows. I certainly don't… at least not yet. You're just going to have to wait until July you greedy bastards.

As always, please consider leaving a review for DRAWING DEAD on Amazon. And if you have any questions or comments, swing by my Facebook group https://www.facebook.com/groups/LogansInsatiableReaders/ or drop me an email (patrick@ptlbooks.com).

You keep reading, and I'll keep writing.

Best,
Patrick
Montreal, 2018

Printed in Great Britain
by Amazon